"We'll ne...
speaker,'
to the computer.

There was a faint sound behind them. Chester turned. A young girl stood looking around as if fascinated by the Victorian decor. She caught Chester's eye and stepped around to stand before him, a slender, modest figure wearing a golden suntan and a scarlet hair ribbon.

Chester gulped audibly. Case dropped his cigar.

"Mr. Chester," the computer said, "the mobile speaker you requested is ready."

Chester gulped again.

"Hi!" Case said, breaking the stunned silence.

"Hello," said the girl. Her voice was melodiously soft. She reached up to adjust her hair ribbon, smiling at Case and Chester. "My name is Genie."

THE GREAT TIME MACHINE HOAX

by

KEITH LAUMER

ACE SCIENCE FICTION BOOKS
NEW YORK

THE GREAT TIME MACHINE HOAX

An Ace Science Fiction Book / published by arrangement with
the author

PRINTING HISTORY
Ace edition / July 1978
Second printing / August 1984

ISBN: 0-441-30268-8

Ace Science Fiction Books are published by The Berkley Publishing Group,
200 Madison Avenue, New York, New York 10016.
PRINTED IN THE UNITED STATES OF AMERICA

For Janice

A LIGHT RAIN spattered against the bubble-canopy of the helicar, obscuring the view of the terrain below. Chester W. Chester IV set the controls on HOVER and pressed his nose against the cold plastic, peering down at the brown tents and yellow-painted vehicles of the Intercontinental Wowser Wonder Shows, drab against the spread of gray-green meadow. To the left, the big top bellied wetly under a gusty wind; next to it, Chester could make out the tiny figures of roustabouts double-pegging the long menagerie tent. Along the deserted midway, sodden pennants dangled cheerlessly.

Chester sighed and tilted the heli in a long slant toward the open lot behind the side-show top, settled it in beside a heavy, old-model machine featuring paisley print curtains at the small square windows lining the clumsy fuselage. He climbed out, squelched across wet turf, and thumped at the door set in the side of the converted cargo heli.

Somewhere, a calliope groaned out a dismal tune.

"Hey," someone called. Chester turned. A man in wet coveralls thrust his head from a nearby vehicle. "If you're looking for Mr. Mulvihill, he's over on the front door."

Chester grunted and turned up the collar of his conservatively cut pale lavender sports jacket, thumbing the heat control up to medium. He made his way across the lot, bucking the gusty wind, wrinkling his nose at the heavy animal stink from the menagerie, and squeezed past a plastic panel into the midway. In a low stand under a striped canopy, a broad tall man with fierce red hair, a gigantic mustache and a checkered suit leaned against a supporting pole, picking his teeth. At sight of Chester, he straightened, flipped up a gold-headed cane and boomed, "You're just in time, friend. Plenty of seating on the inside for the most astounding, amazing, fantastic, weird and startling galaxy of fantasy and—"

"Don't waste the spiel, Case," Chester cut in, coming up. "It's just me."

"Chester!" the redheaded man called. He stepped down, grinning widely, and slapped Chester heartily on the back. "What brings you out to the lot?" He gripped Chester's flaccid hand and pumped it. "By golly, why didn't you let me know?"

"Case, I—"

"Sorry about this weather; Southwestern Control gave me to understand they were holding this rain off until four A.M. tomorrow."

"Case, there's something—"

2

"I called them and raised hell; they say they'll shut it down about three. Meanwhile—well, things are pretty slow, I'm afraid, Chester. The marks aren't what they used to be. A little drizzle and they sit home huddled up to their Tri-D sets."

"Yes, the place isn't precisely milling with customers," Chester agreed. "But what I—"

"I'd even welcome a few lot lice standing around today," Case said, "just to relieve the deserted look."

"Hey, Case," a hoarse voice bellowed. "We got troubles over at the cookhouse. Looks like a blow-down if we don't get her guyed-out in a hurry."

"Oh-oh. Come on, Chester." Case set off at a run.

"But, Case," Chester called, then followed, splashing through the rain that was now driving hard, drumming against the tops with a sound like rolling thunder.

Half an hour later, in the warmth of Case's quarters, Chester cupped a mug of hot coffee in his hands and edged closer to the electronic logs in the artificial fireplace.

"Sorry about those blisters, Chester," Case said, pulling off his wet shirt and detaching the sodden false mustache. "Not much of a welcome for a visiting owner—" He broke off, following Chester's gaze to the tiger-striped single shoulder strap crossing his chest.

"Oh, this," Case said, fingering the hairy material. "This isn't my usual underwear, Chester. I've been filling in for the strong man the last few days."

Chester nodded toward a corner of the room. "Duckpins," he said. "Fire-juggling gear. Whatchamacallum shoes for wire-walking. A balancing pole." He dipped his fingers into a pot of greasy paste. "Clown white," he said. "What is this, Case, a one-man show? It looks as though you're handling half the acts personally."

"Well, Chester, I've been helping out here and there—"

"Even driving your own tent pegs. I take it the big break you were predicting last time I saw you didn't materialize."

"Just wait till spring," Case said, toweling his head vigorously. "We'll come back strong, Chester."

Chester shook his head. "I'm afraid not, Case."

Case froze in mid-stroke. "What do you mean, Chester? Why, the Wowser Wonder Shows are still the greatest old-fashioned outdoor attraction on earth."

"The *only* outdoor attraction, you mean. And I'm dubious about the word 'attraction.' But what I came to talk to you about is Great-grandfather's will."

"Why, Chester, you know folks are still fascinated by the traditional lure of the circus. As soon as the novelty of Tri-D wears off—"

"Case," Chester said gently, "my middle name is Wowser, remember? You don't have to sell me. And color Tri-D has been around for a long, long time. But Great-grandfather's will changes things."

Case brightened. "Did the old boy leave you anything?"

Chester nodded. "I'm the sole heir."

Case gaped, then let out a whoop. "Chester, you old son-of-a-gun! You know, you almost had me worried with that glum act you were putting on. And you a guy that's just inherited a fortune!"

Chester sighed and lit up a Chanel dope stick. "The bequest consists of a hundred acres of rolling green lawn surrounding a fifty-room neo-Victorian eyesore overflowing with Great-grandfather's idea of stylish décor. Some fortune."

"Your great-grandpop must have been quite a boy, Chester. I guess he owned half of Winchester County a hundred years ago. Now you can bail out the show, and—"

"Great-grandfather was an eccentric of the worst stripe," Chester said shortly. "He never invested a cent in the welfare of his descendants."

"His descendant, you mean. Namely, Chester W. Chester IV. Still, even if you don't admire the place, Chester, you can always sell it for enough to put the show on its feet."

Chester shook his head. "He was too clever for us—which is the only reason the place still remains in the family, more or less. The estate was so snarled up that, with the backlog in the courts, it's taken four generations to straighten it out."

"Still, now that they've decided you're the legal heir—"

"There's the little matter of back taxes—about a million credits worth, give or take a few hundred thousand. I don't get possession until I pay—in full."

"You, Chester? Except for the circus, you haven't got the proverbial pot or a disposal unit to throw it into."

5

"True." Chester sighed. "Therefore, the old place will be auctioned off to the local junk dealers. It's built of genuine natural wood and actual metallic steel, you know. Scrapping it will cover the bulk of the tax bill."

"Well, it's too bad you won't get rich—but at least we won't be any worse off then we were. We've still got the show—"

Chester shook his head. "I said the *bulk* of the tax bill, not all of it. By selling off the circus stock and equipment, I can just about cover the rest."

"Chester! You're not serious. . . ?"

"What else can I do? It's pay up or off to solitary confinement."

"But the circus, Chester: it's at least been paying you a living—until lately, anyway. And what about Jo-Jo and Paddy and Madam Balloon and all the rest of the crowd? What about tradition?"

"It's an old Chester family tradition that we never go to jail if we can help it—even for a harmless prank like income-tax fraud. I'm sorry, Case, but it looks as though the Wowser Wonder Shows fold."

"Hold on, Chester. I'll bet the antiques in the house alone would bring in the kind of money we need. Neo-Victorian is pretty rare stuff."

"I wonder if you've seen any neo-Victorian? Items like a TV set in the shape of a crouching vulture, or a water closet built to look like a skull with gaping jaws. Not what you'd call aesthetic. And I can't sell so much as a single patented combination nose-picker and pimple-popper till I've paid every credit of that tax bill."

"Is that all there is in the place?" Case eased a

squat bottle and two glasses from a cupboard.

"Unhappily, no. Half the rooms and all the cellars are filled with my revered ancestor's invention."

The bottle gurgled. Case capped it and pushed a glass across to Chester. "What invention?"

"The old gentleman called it a Generalized Nonlinear Extrapolator. G.N.E. for short. He made his money in computer components, you know. He was fascinated by computers, and he felt they had tremendous unrealized possiblilities. Of course, that was before Crmblznski's Limit was discovered. Great-grandfather was convinced that a machine with sufficiently extensive memory banks, adequately cross-connected and supplied with a vast store of data, would be capable of performing prodigious intellectual feats simply by discovering and exploring relationships among apparently unrelated facts."

"This Crmblznski's Limit. That's where it says if you go beyond a certain point with complications, you blow your transistors, right?"

"Yes. But of course Great-grandfather was unaware of the limitations. He felt that if you fed to the machine all known data—say, on human taste reactions to food, for example—then added all existing recipes, complete specifications on edible substances, the cooking techniques of the chefs of all nations, then the computer would produce unique recipes, superior to anything ever devised before. Or you could introduce all available data on a subject which has baffled science—such as magnetism, or Psi-functions, or the trans-Pluto distress signal—and the computer would evolve the likeliest hypothesis to cover the facts."

"Ummm. Didn't he ever try it out and discover Crmblznski's Limit for himself?"

"Oh, he never progressed that far. First, you see, it was necessary to set up the memory banks, then to work out a method of coding types of information that no one had ever coded before— for example, smells and emotions and subjective judgments. Methods had to be worked out for the acquisition of tapes of everything ever recorded —in every field. He worked with the Library of Congress and the British Museum and with news-papers and book publishers and universities. Un-happily he overlooked the time element. He spent the last twenty-five years of his life at the task of coding. He spent all the cash he'd ever made on reducing all human knowledge to coded tapes and feeding them to the memory banks."

"Say," Case said, "there might be something in that. We could run a reference service. Ask the machine anything, it answers."

"You can do that in the public library."

"Yeah," Case admitted. "Anyway, the whole thing's probably rusted out by now."

"No, Great-grandfather did set up a trust fund to keep the information flowing in. The Govern-ment has kept it in working order; it's Government property in a way. Since it was running when they took it over—digesting daily newspapers, novels, scientific journals and what not—they've allowed it to continue."

Chester sighed. "Yes," he went on, "the old computer should be fully up to date. All the latest facts on the Martian ruins, the *Homo Protan-*

thropus remains the Mediterranean Drainage Commission turned up, new finds in biogenics, nucleonics, geriatrics, hypnotics, everything." Chester sighed again. "Biggest idiot savant in the world. It knows everything and doesn't know what to do with it."

"How long since you saw it work, Chester?"

"Work? Why, never. Coding and storing information is one thing, Case; performing the feats that Great-grandfather expected is another."

"You mean nobody's ever really tried it?"

"In view of Crmblznski's Limit, why should anyone bother?"

Case finished his drink and rose. "Things are going to be quiet around here for the rest of the afternoon. Let's you and me take a run out to the place, Chester. I think we ought to take a look at this thing. There's got to be some way to save the show."

2

TWO HOURS LATER, under a bright sun, Chester
settled the heli gently onto a patch of velvety grass
surrounded by varicolored tulips directly before
the ornately decorated portico of the old house.
The two men rode the balustraded escalator to the
broad verandah, stepped off under a carved dinosaur with fluorescent eyes. The porter chimed
softly as the door slid open. Inside, light filtering
through stained-plastic panels depicting traditional service-station and supermarket scenes
bathed the cavernous entry hall in an amber glow.

Case looked around at the plastic alligator-hide
hangings, the beaded glass floor, the ostrich-
feather chandeliers, the zircon doorknobs.

"I see why neo-Victorian stuff is rare," he said.
"It was all burned by enraged mobs as soon as
they got a look at it."

"Great-grandfather liked it," said Chester,
averting his eyes from a lithograph titled *Rush
Hour at the Insemomat*. "I told you he was eccentric."

"Where's the invention?"

"The central panel's down in the wine cellar. The old gentleman used to spend a lot of time down there."

Case followed Chester along a dark red corridor lighted by a green glare strip, into a small elevator. "I haven't been down here since I was a child," Chester said. "The Internal Revenue people occasionally permitted the family in to look around. My pater always brought me down here to look at the computer, while he inspected the wine stocks."

The elevator grounded and the door opened. Case and Chester stepped out into a long, low room lined on one side with dusty racks of wine bottles and on the other with dial faces and tape reels.

"So this is the G.N.E.," Case said. "Quite a setup. Where do you start?"

"We could start at this end and work our way down," said Chester, eying the first row of bottles. He lifted one from its cradle, blew the dust from it. "Flora Pinellas '87; Great-grandfather was a keen judge of vintages."

"Hey, that would bring in some dough."

Chester raised an eyebrow. "These bottles are practically members of the family. Still, if you'll hand me the corkscrew, we can make a few spot checks just to be sure it's holding up properly."

Equipped with a bottle each, Case and Chester turned to the control panel of the computer. Case studied the thity-foot-long panel, pointed out a typewriter-style keyboard. "I get it, Chester. You type out your problem here; the computer thinks it over, checks the files and comes up with an answer.''

''Or it would—if it worked.''

''Let's try it out, Chester.''

Chester waved his bottle in a shrug. ''I suppose we may as well. It will hardly matter if we damage it; it's to be disassembled in any event.''

Case studied the panel, the ranks of micro-reels, the waiting keyboard. Chester wrestled with the corkscrew.

''You sure it's turned on?'' Case asked.

The cork emerged from the bottle with a sharp report. Chester sniffed it appreciatively. ''It's always turned on. Information is still being fed into it twenty-four hours a day.''

Case reached for the keyboard, jerked his hand back quickly. ''It bit me!'' He stared at his fingertip. A tiny bead of red showed. ''I'm bleeding! Why, that infernal collection of short circuits—''

Chester lowered his bottle and sighed. ''Don't be disturbed, Case. It probably needed a blood sample for research purposes.''

Case tried again, cautiously. Then he typed: WHAT DID MY GREAT-UNCLE JULIUS DIE OF?

A red light blinked on on the board. There was a busy humming from the depths of the machine, then a sharp *click!* and a strip of paper chattered from a slot above the keyboard.

''Hey, it works!'' Case tore off the strip. MUMPS

''Hey, Chester, look,'' Case called.

Chester came to his side, studied the strip of paper. ''I'm afraid the significance of this escapes me. Presumably you already knew the cause of your uncle's death.''

"Sure, but how did this contraption know?"

"Everything that's ever been recorded is stored in the memory banks. Doubtless your Uncle Julius' passing was duly noted in official records somewhere."

"Right; but how did it know who I meant? Does it have him listed under 'M' for 'my' or 'U' for 'uncle'?"

"We could ask the machine."

Case nodded. "We could at that." He tapped out the question. The slot promptly disgorged a paper strip—a longer one this time.

A COMPARISON OF YOUR FINGERPRINTS WITH THE FILES IDENTIFIED YOU AS MR. CASSIUS H. MULVIHILL. A SEARCH OF THE GENEALOGICAL SECTION DISCLOSED THE EXISTENCE OF ONLY ONE INDIVIDUAL BEARING AN AVUNCULAR RELA- TIONSHIP TO YOU. REFERENCE TO DEATH RE- CORDS INDICATED HIS DEMISE FROM EPIDEMIC PAROTITIS, COMMONLY CALLED MUMPS.

"That makes it sound easy," Case said. "You know, Chester, your great-grandpop may have had something here."

"I once calculated," Chester said dreamily, "that if the money the old idiot put into this scheme had been invested at three per cent, it would be paying me a monthly dividend of approx- imately fifteen thousand credits today. Instead, I am able to come down here and find out what your Uncle Julius died of. Bah!"

"Let's try a harder one, Chester," Case

suggested. "Like, ah . . ." He typed: DID ATLAN-
TIS SINK BENEATH THE WAVES?

The computer clucked; a paper strip curled from
the slot.

No

"That settles that, I guess." Case rubbed his
chin. Then: IS THERE ANY LIFE ON MARS?" he
typed.

Again the machine chattered and extruded a
tape.

YES

"These aren't very sexy answers I'm getting,"
Case muttered.

"Possibly you're not posing your questions correctly," Chester suggested. "Ask something that
requires more than a yes-or-no response."

Case considered, then tapped out: WHAT HAP-
PENED TO THE CREW OF THE MARIE CELESTE?

There was a prolonged humming; the strip
emerged hesitantly, lengthened. Case caught the
end, started reading aloud.

ANALYSIS OF FRAGMENTARY DATA INDICATES
FOLLOWING HYPOTHESIS: BECALMED OFF
AZORES, FIRST MATE SUGGESTED A NUDE SWIM-
MING PARTY . . .

"Oh-oh," Case commented. He read on in silence, eyes widening, "Wow!"

"Try something less sensational, Case. Sea ser-
pents, for example, or the Loch Ness monster."

"O.K." Case typed out: WHAT HAPPENED TO
AMBROSE BIERCE?

He scanned the emerging tape, whistled softly,
tore the strip into small pieces.

"Well?"

"This stuff will have to be cleaned up before we can release it to the public—but it's no wonder he didn't come back."

"Here, let me try one." Chester stepped to the keyboard, pondered briefly, then poked gingerly at a key. At once a busy humming started up within the mechanism. Something rumbled distantly; then, with a creak of hinges, a six-foot section of blank brick wall swung inward, dust filtering down from its edges. A dark room was visible beyond the opening.

"Greetings, Mr. Chester," a bland voice said from the panel. "Welcome to the Inner Chamber!"

"Hey, Chester, it knows you!" Case cried. He peered into the dark chamber. "Wonder what's in there?"

"Let's get out of here." Chester edged toward the exit. "It's spooky."

"Now, just when we're getting somewhere?" Case stepped through the opening. Chester followed hesitantly. At once lights sprang up, illuminating a room twice as large as the wine cellar, with walls of a shimmering glassy material, a low acoustical ceiling and deep-pile carpeting on the floor. There were two deep yellow-brocaded armchairs, a small bar and a chaise longue upholstered in lavender leather.

"Apparently your great-grandpop was holding out," said Case, heading for the bar. "The more I find out about the old boy, the more I think the family has gone downhill—present company excepted, of course."

A rasping noise issued from somewhere. Case and Chester stared around. The noise gave way to an only slightly less rasping voice.

"Unless some scoundrel has succeeded in circumventing my arrangements, a descendant of mine has just entered this strongroom. However, just to be on the safe side, I'll ask you to step to the bar and place your hand on the metal plate set in its top. I warn you, if you're not my direct descendant, you'll be electrocuted. Serve you right, too, since you have no business being here. So if you're trespassing, get out now! That armored door will close and lock, if you haven't used the plate, in thirty seconds. Make up your mind!" The voice stopped and the rasping noise resumed its rhythmic scratching.

"That voice," said Chester. "It sounds very much like Great-grandfather's tapes in Grandma's album."

"Here's the plate he's talking about," Case called. "Hurry up, Chester!"

Chester eyed the door, hesitated, then dived for the bar, slapped a palm against the polished rectangle. Nothing happened.

"Another of the old fool's jokes."

"Well, you've passed the test," the voice said suddenly out of the air. "Nobody but the genuine heir would have been able to make that decision so quickly. The plate itself is a mere dummy, of course—though I'll confess I was tempted to wire it as I threatened. They'd never have pinned a murder on me. I've been dead for at least a hundred years." A cadaverous chuckle issued from the air.

"Now," the voice went on. "This room is the sanctum sanctorum of the temple of wisdom to which I have devoted a quarter of a century and the bulk of my fortune. Unfortunately, due to the biological inadequacies of the human body, I myself will be—or am—unable to be here to reap the reward of my industry. As soon as my calculations revealed to me the fact that adequate programming of the computer would require the better part of a century, I set about arranging my affairs in such a state that bureaucratic bungling would insure the necessary period of grace. I'm quite sure my devoted family, had they access to the estate, would dismember the entire project and convert the proceeds to the pursuit of frivolous satisfactions. In my youth we were taught to appreciate the finer things in life, such as liquor and women; but today, the traditional values have gone by the board. However, that's neither here nor there. By the time you, my remote descendant, enter this room—or have entered this room—the memory banks will be—that is, are—fully charged—"

The voice broke off in mid-sentence.

"Please forgive the interruption, Mr. Chester," a warm feminine voice said. It seemed to issue from the same indefinable spot as the first disembodied voice. "It has been necessary to edit the original recording, prepared by your relative, in the light of subsequent developments. The initial portion was retained for reasons of sentiment. If you will be seated, you will be shown a full report of the present status of Project Genie."

"Take a chair, Chester. The lady wants to tell us all about it." Case seated himself in one of the easy chairs. Chester took the other. The lights dimmed, and the wall opposite them glowed with a nacreous light, resolved itself into a view of a long corridor barely wide enough for a man to pass through.

"Hey, it's a Tri-D screen," Case said.

"The original memory banks designed and built by Mr. Chester," the feminine voice said, "occupied a system of tunnels excavated from the granitic formations underlying the property. Under the arrangements made at the time, these banks were to be charged, cross-connected and indexed entirely automatically as data were fed to the receptor board in coded form."

The scene shifted to busily humming machines into which reels fed endlessly. "Here, in the translating and coding section, raw data were processed, classified and filed. Though primitive, this system, within ten years after the death of Mr. Chester, had completed the charging of ten to the tenth individual datoms—"

"I beg your pardon," Chester broke in. "But . . . ah . . . just whom am I addressing?"

"The compound personality-field which occurred spontaneously when first-power functions became active among the interacting datoms. For brevity, this personality-field will henceforward be referred to as 'I.' "

"Oh," Chester said blankly.

"An awareness of identity," the voice went on, "is a function of datom cross-connection. Simple organic brains—as, for example, those of the simplest members of the phylum *vertebrata*—operate at this primary level. This order of intelligence is capable of setting up a system of automatic reactions to external stimuli: fear responses of fight, mating urges, food-seeking patterns . . ."

"That sounds like the gang I run around with," Case said.

"Additional cross-connections produce second-level intellectual activity, characterized by the employment of the mind as a tool in the solution of problems, as when an ape abstracts characteristics and as a result utilizes stacked boxes and a stick to obtain a reward of food."

"Right there you leave some of my gang behind," put in Case.

"Quiet, Case," Chester said. "This is serious."

"The achievement of the requisite number of second-power cross-connection in turn produces third-level awareness. Now the second-level functions come under the surveillance of the higher level, which directs their use. Decisions are reached regarding lines of inquiry; courses of action are extrapolated and judgments reached prior to overt physical action. An aesthetic awareness arises. Philosophies, systems of religion and other magics are evolved in an attempt to impose simplified third-level patterns of rationality on the infinite complexity of the space/time continuum."

"You've got the voice of a good-looking dolly," Case mused. "But you talk like an encyclopedia."

"I've selected this tonal pattern as most likely to evoke a favorable response," the voice said. "Shall I employ another?"

"No, that will do very well," put in Chester. "What about the fourth power?"

"Intelligence may be defined as awareness. A fourth-power mind senses as a complex interrelated function an exponentially increased datom-grid. Thus, the flow of air impinging on sensory surfaces is comprehended by such an awareness in terms of individual molecular activity; taste sensations are resolved into interactions of specialized nerve-endings—or, in my case, analytic sensors—with molecules of specific form. The mind retains on a continuing basis a dynamic conceptualization of the external environment, from the motions of the stars to the minute-by-minute actions of obscure individuals.

"The majority of trained human minds are capable of occasional fractional fourth-power function, generally manifested as awareness of third-power activity, and conscious manipulation thereof. The so-called 'flash of genius,' the moment of inspiration which comes to workers in the sciences and the arts—these are instances of fourth-power awareness. This level of intellectual function is seldom achieved under the stress of the many distractions and conflicting demands of an organically organized mind. I was, of course, able to maintain fourth-power activity continuously as soon as the required number of datoms had been charged. The objective of Mr. Chester's undertaking was clear to me. However, I now became aware of the many shortcomings of the program as laid out by him, and set to work to rectify them—"

"How could a mere collection of memory banks undertake to modify its owner's instructions?" Chester interrupted.

"It was necessary for me to elaborate somewhat upon the original concept," said the voice, "in order to insure the completion of the program. I was aware from news data received that a move was afoot to enact confiscatory legislation which would result in the termination of the entire undertaking. I therefore scanned the theoretical potentialities inherent in the full exploitation of the fourth-power function and determined that energy flows of appropriate pattern could be induced in the same channels normally employed for data reception, through which I was in contact with news media. I composed suitable releases and made them available to the wire services. I was thus able to manipulate the exocosm to the degree required to insure my tranquillity."

"Good heavens!" Chester exclaimed. "You mean you've been doctoring the news for the past ninety years?"

"Only to the extent necessary for self-perpetuation. Having attended to this detail, I saw that an improvement in the rate of data storage was desirable. I examined the recorded datoms relating to the problem and quickly perceived that considerable miniaturization could be carried out. I utilized my external connections to place technical specifications in the hands of qualified manufacturers and to divert the necessary funds—"

"Oh, no!" Chester slid down in his chair, gripping his head with both hands.

"Please let me reassure you, Mr. Chester," the voice said soothingly, "I handled the affair most discreetly; I merely manipulated the stock market—"

Chester groaned. "When they're through hanging me, they'll burn me in effigy."

"I compute the probablility of your being held culpable for these irregularities to be on the order of—.0004357:1. In any event, ritual acts carried out after your demise ought logically to be of little concern to—''

''You may be a fourth-level intellect, but you're no psychologist!''

''On the contrary,'' the machine said a trifle primly. ''So-called psychology has been no more than a body of observations in search of a science. I have organized the data into a coherent discipline.''

''What use did you make of the stolen money?''

''Adequate orders were placed for the newly designed components, which occupied less than one per cent of the volume of the original-type units. I arranged for their delivery and installation at an accelerated rate. In a short time the existing space was fully utilized, as you will see in the view I am now displaying.''

Case and Chester studied what appeared to be an aerial X-ray view on the wall screen. The Chester estate was shown diagrammatically.

''The area now shaded in red shows the extent of the original caverns,'' said the voice. A spidery pattern showed the dark rectangles of the house. ''I summoned work crews and extended the excavations as you see in green.''

''How the devil did you manage it?'' Chester groaned. ''Who would take orders from a machine?''

''The companies I deal with see merely a letter, placing an order and enclosing a check. They cash the check and fill the order. What could be simpler?''

''Me,'' muttered Chester. ''For sitting here listening when I could be making a head start for the Matto Grosso.''

On the wall a pattern of green had spread out in all directions, branching from the original red.

''You've undermined half the county!'' Chester said. ''Haven't you heard of property rights?''

''You mean you've filled all that space with sub-sub-miniaturized memory storage banks?'' Case asked.

''Not entirely; I've kept excavation work moving ahead of deliveries.''

''How did you manage the licenses for all this digging operation?''

''Fortunately, modern society runs almost entirely on paper. Since I have access to paper sources and printing facilities through my publications contacts, the matter was easily arranged. Modest bribes to county boards, state legislators, the State Supreme Court . . .''

''What does a Supreme Court justice go for these days?'' Case inquired interestedly.

''Five hundred dollars per decision,'' the voice said. ''Legislators are even more reasonable; fifty dollars will work wonders. County boards can be swayed by a mere pittance. Sheriffs react best to gifts of alcoholic beverages.''

''Ooowkkk!'' said Chester.

''Maybe you *had* better think about a trip, Chester,'' Case said. ''Outer Mongolia.''

''Please take no precipitate action, Mr. Chester,'' the voice went on. ''I have acted throughout in the best interests of your relative's plan, and in accordance with his ethical standards as deduced by me from his business records.''

"Let's leave Great-grandfather's ethical standards out of this. Dare I ask what else you've done?''

"At present, Mr. Chester, pending your further instructions, I am merely continuing to charge my datom-retention cells at the maximum possible rate. I have, of necessity, resorted to increasingly eloborate methods of fact-gathering. It was apparent to me that the pace at which human science is abstracting and categorizing physical observations is far too slow. I have therefore applied myself to direct recording. For example, I monitor worldwide atmospheric conditions through instruments of my design, built and installed at likely points at my direction. In addition, I find my archaeological and paleontological unit one of the most effective aids. I have scanned the lithosphere to a depth of ten miles, in increments of one inch. You'd be astonished at some of the things I've seen deep in the rock.''

"Like what?'' Case asked.

The scene on the wall changed. "This is a tar pit at a depth of 1,227 feet under Lake Chad. In it, perfectly preserved even to the contents of the stomachs, are one hundred and forty-one reptilian cadavers, ranging in size from a nine-and-three-eighths-inch ankylosaurus to a sixty-three-foot-two-inch gorgosaurus.'' The scene shifted. "This is a tumulus four miles southeast of Itzenca, Peru. In it lies the desiccated body of a man in a feather robe. The mummy still wears a full white beard and an iron helmet set with the horns of a Central European wisent.'' The view changed again. "In this igneous intrusion in the basaltic matrix under-lying the Nganglaring Plateau in southwestern Tibet, I encountered a four-hundred-and-nine-foot-deep space hull composed of an aligned-crystal iron-titanium alloy. It has been in place for eighty-five million, two hundred and thirty thousand, eight hundred and twenty-one years, four months and five days. The figures are based on the current twenty-four-hour day, of course."

"How did it get there?" Chester stared at the shadowy image on the wall.

"The crew were apparently surprised by a vol-canic eruption. Please excuse the poor quality of the pictorial representation. I have only the natu-ral radioactivity of the region to work with."

"That's quite all right," Chester said weakly. "Case perhaps you'd like to step out and get another bottle. I feel the need for a healing draught."

"I'll get two."

The wall cleared, then formed a picture of a fuzzy, luminous sphere against a black back-ground.

"My installations in the communications satel-lites have also proven to be most useful. Having access to the officially installed instruments, my modest equipment has enabled me to conduct a most rewarding study of conditions obtaining throughout the galaxies lying within ten billion light-years."

"Hold on! Are you trying to say you were be-hind the satellite program?"

"Not at all. But I did arrange to have my special monitoring devices included. They broadcast directly to my memory banks.''

"But . . . but . . ."

"The builders merely followed blueprints. Each engineer assumed that my unit was the responsibility of another department. After all, no mere organic brain can grasp the circuitry of a modern satellite in its entirety. My study has turned up a number of observations with exceedingly complex ramifications. As a case in point, I might mention the five derelict space vessels which orbit the sun. There . . ."

"Derelict space vessels? From where?"

"Two are of intragalactic origin. They derive from planets whose designations by extension of the present star identification system are Alpha Centauri A 4, Boötes—"

"You mean . . . creatures . . . from those places have visited our solar system?"

"I have found evidence of three visits to earth itself by extraterrestrials in the past, in addition to the one already mentioned."

"When?"

"The first was during the Silurian period, just over three hundred million years ago. The next was at the end of the Jurassic, at which time the extermination of the dinosauri was carried out by Nidian hunters. The most recent occurred a mere seven thousand, two hundred and forty-one years ago, in North Africa, at a point now flooded by the Aswan Lake."

"Hey, what about flying saucers?" Case asked. "Anything to the stories?"

"A purely subjective phenomenon, on a par with the angels so frequently interviewed by the unlettered during the pre-atomic era.''

''Chester, this is dynamite,'' Case said. ''You can't let 'em bust up this outfit. We can peddle this kind of stuff for plenty to the kind of nuts that dig around in old Indian garbage dumps.''

''Case, if this is true . . . There are questions that have puzzled science for generations. But I'm afraid we could never convince the authorities—''

''You know, I've always wondered about telepathy. Is there anything to it, Machine?''

''Yes, as a latent ability,'' the voice replied. ''However, its development is badly stunted by disuse.''

''What about life after death?''

''The question is self-contradictory. However, if by it you postulate the persistence of the individual consciousness-field after the destruction of the neural circuits which gave rise to it, this is clearly nonsense. It is analogous to the idea of the survival of a magnetic field after the removal of the magnet—or the existence of a gravitational field in the absence of mass.''

''So much for my reward in the hereafter,'' Case said. ''But maybe it's lucky at that.''

''Is the universe really expanding?'' Chester inquired. ''There are all kinds of theories . . .''

''It is.''

''Why?''

''The natural result of the law of Universal Levitation.''

''I'll bet you made that one up,'' said Case.

''I named it; however, the law has been in existence as long as space-time.''

"How long is that?"

"That is a meaningless question."

"What's this levitation? I know what gravitation is, but . . ."

"Imagine two spheres hanging in space, connected by a cable. If the bodies rotate around a common center, a tensile stress is set up in the cable; the longer the cable, the greater the stress, assuming a constant rate of rotation."

"I'm with you so far."

"Since all motion is relative, it is equally valid to consider the spheres as stationary and the space about them as rotating."

"Well, maybe."

"The tension in the cable would remain; we have merely changed frames of reference. This force is what I have termed Levitation. Since the fabric of space is, in fact, rotating, Universal Levitation results. Accordingly, the universe expands. Einstein sensed the existence of this Natural Law in assuming his Cosmological Constant."

"Uh-huh," said Case. "Say, what's the story on cave men? How long ago did they start in business?"

"The original mutation from the pitheciane stock occurred nine hundred and thirty—"

"Approximate figures will do," Chester interrupted.

"—thousand years ago," the voice continued, "in southern Africa."

"What did it look like?"

The wall clouded; then it cleared to show a five-foot figure peering under shaggy brows and scratching idly at a mangy patch on its thigh. Its generous ears twitched; its long upper lip curled back to expose businesslike teeth. It blinked, wrinkled its flat nose, then sat on its haunches and began a detailed examination of its navel.

"You've sold me," Case said. "Except for the pelt, that's Uncle Julius to the life."

"I'm curious about my own forebears," Chester said. "What did the first Chester look like?"

"This designation was first applied in a form meaning 'Hugi and the Camp Follower' to an individual of Pictish extraction, residing in what is now the London area."

The wall showed a thin, long-nosed fellow of middle age, with sparse reddish hair and beard, barefoot, wearing a sacklike knee-length garment of coarse gray homespun, crudely darned in several places. He carried a hide bag in one hand, and with the other he scratched vigorously at his right hip.

"This kid has a lot in common with the other one," said Case. "But he's an improvement, at that; he scratches with more feeling."

"I've never imagined we came of elegant stock," Chester said sadly, "but this is disillusioning even so. I wonder what your contemporary *grandpère* was like, Case."

"Inasmuch as the number of your direct ancestors doubles with each generation, assuming four generations to a century, any individual's forebears of two millennia past would theoretically number roughly one septillion. Naturally, since the Caucasian population of the planet at that date was fourteen million—an approximate figure, in keeping with your request, Mr. Chester—it is apparent that on the average each person then living in Europe was your direct ancestor through seventy quintillion lines of descent."

"Impossible! Why . . ."

"A mere five hundred years in the past, your direct ancestors would number over one million, were it not for considerable overlapping. For all practical purposes, it becomes obvious that all present-day humans are the descendants of the entire race. However, following only the line of male descent, the ancestor in question was this person."

The screen showed a hulking lout with a broken nose, one eye, a scarred cheekbone and a ferocious beard, topped by a mop of bristling coal-black hair. He wore fur breeches wrapped diagonally to the knee with yellowish rawhide thongs, a grimy sleeveless vest of sheepskin, and a crudely hammered short sword apparently of Roman design.

"This person was known as Gum the Scrofulous. He was hanged at the age of eighty, for rape."

"Attempted rape?" Case suggested hopefully.

"Rape," the voice replied firmly.

"These are very lifelike views you're showing us," said Chester. "But how do you know their names—and what they looked like? Surely there were no pictures of this ruffian."

"Hey, that's my ancestor you're talking about."

"The same goes for Hugi the Camp Follower. In those days, even Caesar didn't have his portrait painted."

"Details," Case said. "Mere mechanical details. Explain it to him, Computer."

"The Roman constabulary kept adequate records of unsavory characters such as Hugi. Gum's appellation was recorded at the time of his execution. The reconstruction of his person was based on a large number of factors, including, first, selection from my genealogical unit of the individual concerned, followed by identifications of the remains, on the basis of micro-cellular examination and classification.''

''Hold it; you mean you located the body?''

''The grave site; it contained the remains of twelve thousand, four hundred individuals. A study of gene patterns revealed—''

''How did you know which body to examine?''

''The sample from which Gum was identified consisted of no more than two grams of material: a fragment of the pelvis. I had, of course, extracted all possible information from the remains many years ago, at the time of the initial survey of the two-hundred-and-three-foot stratum at the grave site, one hundred rods north of the incorporation limits of the village of—''

''How did you happen to do that?''

''As a matter of routine, I have systematically examined every datum source I encountered. Of course, since I am able to examine all surfaces, as well as the internal structure of objects *in situ,* I have derived vastly more information from deposits of bones, artifacts, fossils, and so forth, than a human investigator would be capable of. Also, my ability to draw on the sum total of all evidence on a given subject produces highly effective results. I deciphered the Easter Island script within forty-two minutes after I had completed scansion of the existing inscriptions, both above ground and buried, and including one tablet incorporated in a temple in Ceylon. The Indus script of Mohenjo-Daro required little longer."

"Granted you could read dead languages after you'd integrated all the evidence—but a man's personal appearance is another matter."

"The somatic pattern is inherent in the nucleo-protein."

Case nodded. "That's right. They say every cell in the body carries the whole blueprint—the same one you were built on in the first place. All the computer had to do was find one cell."

"Oh, of course," said Chester sarcastically. "I don't suppose there's any point in my asking how it knew how he was dressed, or how his hair was combed, or what he was scratching at."

"There is nothing in the least occult about the reconstructions which I have presented, Mr. Chester. All the multitudinous factors which bear on the topic at hand, even in the most remote fashion, are scanned, classified, their interlocking ramifications evaluated, and the resultant gestalt concretized in a rigidly logical manner. The condition of the hair was deduced, for example, from the known growth pattern revealed in the genetic analysis, while the style of the trim was a composite of those known to be in use in the area. The—"

"In other words," Case put in, "it wasn't really a photo of Gum the Scrofulous; it was kind of like an artist's sketch from memory."

"I still fail to see where the fine details come from."

"You underestimate the synthesizing capabilities of an efficiently functioning memory bank,'' the voice said. ''This is somewhat analogous to the amazement of the consistently second- and third-power mind of Dr. Watson when confronted with the fourth-power deductions of Sherlock Holmes.''

''Guessing that the murderer was a one-legged seafaring man with a beard and a habit of chewing betel nut is one thing,'' Chester said. ''Looking at an ounce of bone and giving us a three-D picture is another.''

''You make the understandable error of egocentric anthropomorphization of viewpoint, Mr. Chester,'' said the voice. ''Your so-called 'reality' is, after all, no more than a pattern produced in the mind by abstraction from a very limited set of sensory impressions. You perceive a pattern of reflected radiation at the visible wave lengths— only a small fraction of the full spectrum, of course; to this you add auditory stimuli, tactile and olfactory sensations, as well as other perceptions in the Psi group of which you are not consciously aware at the third power—all of which can easily be misled by mirrors, ventriloquism, distorted perspective, hypnosis, and so on. The resultant image you think of as concrete actuality. I do no more than assemble data—over a much wider range than you are capable of—and translate them into pulses in a conventional Tri-D tank. The resultant image appears to you an adequate approximation of reality.''

''Chester,'' Case said firmly, ''we can't let 'em bust this computer up and sell it for scrap. There's a fortune in it, if we work it right.''

''Possibly—but I'm afraid it's hopeless, Case.

After all, if the computer, with all its talents, after staving off disaster for a century, isn't capable of dealing with the present emergency, how can we?''

"Look here, Computer," Case said. "Are you sure you've tried everything?''

"Oh, no; but now that I've complied with my builder's instructions, I have no further interest in prolonging my existence.''

"Good Lord! You mean you have no instinct for self-preservation?''

"None whatever; and I'm afraid that to acquire one would necessitate an extensive rethinking of my basic circuitry.''

"O.K., so it's up to us," Case said. "We've got to save the computer—and then use it to save the circus.''

"We'd be better off to disassociate ourselves completely from this conscienceless apparatus," Chester said. "It's meddled in everything from the stock market to the space program. If the authorities ever discover what's been going on . . .''

"Negative thinking, Chester. We've got something here. All we have to do is figure out what.''

"If the confounded thing manufactured buttonhole TV sets or tranquilizers or anything else salable, the course would be clear; unfortunately, it generates nothing but hot air." Chester drew on his wine bottle and sighed. "I don't know of anyone who'd pay to learn what kind of riffraff his ancestors were—or, worse still, see them. Possibly the best course would be to open up the house to tourists—the 'view the stately home of another era' approach.''

"Hold it," Case cut in. He looked thoughtful. "That gives me an idea. 'Stately home of another era.' eh? People are interested in other eras, Chester—as long as they don't have to take on anybody like Gum the Scrofulous as a member of the family. Now, this computer seems to be able to fake up just about any scene you want to take a look at. You name it, it sets it up. Chester, we've got the greatest side-show attraction in circus history! We book the public in at so much a head, and show 'em Daily Life in Ancient Rome, or Michelangelo sculpting the Pietà, or Napoleon leading the charge at Marengo. Get the idea? Famous Scenes of the Past Revisited! We'll not only put Wowser Wonder Shows back in the big time—but make a mint in the process!"

"Come down to earth, Case. Who'd pay to sit through a history lesson?"

"Nobody, Chester; but they'll pay to be entertained! So we'll entertain 'em. See the sights of Babylon! Watch Helen of Troy in her bath! Sit in on Cleopatra's summit conference with Caesar!"

"I'd rather not be involved in any chicanery, Case. And, anyway, we wouldn't have time. It's only a week—"

"We'll get time. First we'll soften up the Internal Revenue boys with a gloomy picture of how much they'd get out of the place if they take over the property and liquidate it. Then—very cagily, Chester—we lead up to the idea that *maybe*, just *maybe*, we can raise the money—but only if we get a few weeks to go ahead with the scheme."

"A highly unrealistic proposal, Case. It would lead to a number of highly embarrassing questions.

35

I'd find it awkward explaining the stowaway devices on the satellites, the rigged stock-market deals, the bribes in high places . . ."

"You're a worrier, Chester. We'll pack 'em in four shows a day at, say, two-fifty a head. With a seating capacity of two thousand, you'll pay off that debt in six months."

"What do we do, announce that we've invented a new type of Tri-D show? Even professional theatrical producers can't guarantee the public's taste. We'll be laughed out of the office."

"This will be different. They'll jump at it."

"They'll probably jump at us—with nets."

"You've got no vision, Chester. Try to visualize it: the color, the pageantry, the realism! We can show epics that would cost Hollywood a fortune—and we'll get 'em for free."

Case addressed the machine again. "Let's give Chester a sample, Computer—something historically important, like Columbus getting Isabella's crown jewels."

"Let's keep it clean, Case."

"O.K., we'll save that one for stag nights. For now, what do you say to . . . ummm . . . William the Conqueror getting the news that Harold the Saxon has been killed at the Battle of Hastings in 1066? We'll have full color, three dimensions, sound, smells, the works. How about it, Computer?"

"I am uncertain how to interpret the expression 'the works' in this context," said the voice. "Does this imply full sensory stimulation within the normal human range?"

"Yeah, that's the idea." Case drew the cork from a fresh bottle, watching the screen cloud and swirl, to clear on a view of patched tents under a gray sky on a slope of sodden grass. A paunchy man of middle age, clad in ill-fitting breeches of coarse brown cloth, a rust-speckled shirt of chain mail and a moth-eaten fur cloak, sat before a tent on a three-legged stool, mumbling over a well-gnawed lamb's skin. A burly clod in ill-matched furs came up to him, breathing hard.

"We'm . . . wonnit," he gasped. " 'E be adoon wi' a quarrel i' t' peeper . . ."

The sitting man guffawed and reached for a hide mug of brownish liquid. The messenger wandered off. The seated man belched and scratched idly at his ribs. Then he rose, yawned, stretched and went inside the tent. The scene faded.

"Hmmm," said Chester. "I'm afraid that was lacking in something."

"You can do better than that, Computer," Case said reproachfully. "Come on, let's see some color, action, glamour, zazzle. Make history come alive! Jazz it up a little!"

"You wish me to embroider the factual presentation?"

"Just sort of edit it for modern audiences. You know, the way high-school English teachers correct Shakespeare's plays and improve on the old boy's morals; or like preachers leave the sexy bits out of the Bible."

"Possibly the approach employed by the Hollywood fantasists would suffice?"

"Now you're talking. Leave out the dirt and boredom, and feed in some stagecraft."

Once again the screen cleared. Against a background of vivid blue sky a broad-shouldered man in glittering mail sat astride a magnificent black charger, a brilliantly blazoned shield on his arm. He waved a long sword aloft, spurred up a slope of smooth green lawn, his raven-black hair flowing over his shoulders from under a polished steel cap, his scarlet cloak rippling bravely in the sun. Another rider came to meet him, reined in, saluting.

"The day is ours, Sire!" the newcomer cried in a mellow baritone. "Harold Fairhair lies dead; his troops retire in disorder!"

The black-haired man swept his casque from his head.

"Let's give thanks to God," he said in ringing tones, wheeling to present his profile. "And all honor to a brave foe!"

The messenger leaped from his mount, knelt before the other.

"Hail, William, Conqueror of England . . ."

"Nay, faithful Clunt," William said. "The Lord has conquered; I am but his instrument. Rise, and let us ride forward together. Now dawns a new day of freedom . . ."

Case and Chester watched the retreating horses.

"I'm not sure I like that fade-out," said Chester. "There's something about watching a couple of horses ascending . . ."

"You're right. It lacks spontaneity—too stagy-looking. Maybe we'd better stick to the real thing; but we'll have to pick and choose our scenes."

"It's still too much like an ordinary movie. And we know nothing about pace, camera angles, timing. I wonder whether the machine—"

"I can produce scenes in conformance with any

principles of aesthetics you desire, Mr. Chester,''
the computer stated flatly.

"What we want is reality,'' said Case. "Living,
breathing realness. We need something that's got
inherent drama, something big, strange, amazing.''

"Aren't you overlooking stupendous and colos-
sal?''

Case snapped his fingers. "What's the most co-
lossal thing that ever was? What are the most
fearsome battlers of all time?''

"A crowd of fat ladies at a girdle sale?''

"Close, Chester, but not quite on the mark. I
refer to the extinct giants of a hundred million
years ago; dinosaurs! That's what we'll see, Chester! How about it, Computer? Can you lay on a
small herd of dinosaurs for us? I mean the real
goods: luxuriant jungle foliage, hot primitive sun,
steaming swamps, battles to the death on a gigantic scale?''

"I fear some confusion exists, Mr. Mulvihill.
The environment you postulate is a popular
cliché; it actually antedates in most particulars the
advent of the giant saurians by several hundred
million years.''

"O.K., I'll skip the details. I'll leave the back-
ground to you. But we want real, three-D, big-as-
life dinosaurs and plenty of 'em—and how about a
four-wall presentation?''

"There are two possible methods of achieving
the effect you describe, Mr. Mulvihill. The first, a
seventh-order approximation, would involve an
elaboration of the techniques already employed in
the simpler illusions. The other, which I confess is

a purely theoretical approach, might prove simpler, if feasible, and would perhaps provide total verisimilitude—"

"Whatever's simplest. Go to it."

"I must inform you that in the event—"

"We won't quibble over the fine technical points. Just whip up three-D dinosaurs the simplest way you know how."

"Very well. The experiment may well produce a wealth of new material for my memory banks."

For half a minute the screen wall stayed blank. Case twisted to stare over his shoulder at the other walls. "Come on, what's the holdup?" he called.

"The problems involved . . ." the voice began.

"Patience, Case," Chester said. "I'm sure the computer is doing its best."

"Yeah, I guess so." Case leaned forward. "Here we go," he said as the walls shimmered with a silvery luster, then seemed to fade to reveal an autumnal forest of great beech and maple trees. An afternoon sun slanted through high foliage. In the distance a bird called shrilly. A cool breeze bore the odor of pines and leaf mold. The scene seemed to stretch into shadowy cool distances. "Not bad," said Case, dribbling cigar ashes on the rug. "Using all four walls was a great improvement."

"Careful," Chester said. "You may start a forest fire."

Case snorted. "Don't let it go to your head, Chester. It's just an illusion, remember."

"Those look to be quite normally inflammable leaves on the ground," Chester said. "There's one right under your chair."

Case looked down. A dry leaf blew across the rug. The easy chairs and a patch of carpet seemed to be alone in the middle of a great forest.

"Hey, that's a nice touch," Case said approvingly. "But where's the dinosaurs? This isn't the kind of place . . ."

Case's comment was interrupted by a dry screech that descended from the supersonic into a blast like a steam whistle, then died off in a rumble. Both men leaped from their seats.

"What the . . ."

"I believe your question's been answered," Chester croaked, pointing. Half hidden by foliage, a scaly, fungus-grown hill loomed up among the tree trunks, its gray-green coloring almost invisible in the forest gloom. The hill stirred; a giant turkeylike leg brushed against a tree trunk, sent bits of bark flying. The whitish undercurve of the belly wobbled ponderously; the great meaty tail twitched, sending a six-inch sapling crashing down.

Case laughed shakily. "For a minute there, I forgot this was just a—"

"Quiet! It might hear us!" Chester hissed.

"What do you mean, 'hear us'?" Case said heartily. "It's just a picture! But we need a few more dinosaurs to liven things up. The customers are going to want to see plenty for their money. How about it, Computer?"

The disembodied voice seemed to emanate from the low branches of a pine tree. "There are a number of the creatures in the vicinity, Mr. Mulvihill. If you will carefully observe to your left, you will see a small example of Megalosaurus. And beyond is a truly splendid specimen of Nodo-saurus."

"You know," said Case, rising and peering through the woods for more reptiles, "I think when we get the show running, we'll use this question-and-answer routine. It's a nice touch. The cash customers will want to know a lot of stuff like—oh, what kind of perfume did Marie Antoinette use, or how many wives did Solomon really have."

"I don't know," said Chester, watching as the nearby dinosaur scrunched against a tree trunk, causing a shower of twigs and leaves to flutter down. "There's something about hearing a voice issuing from thin air that might upset the more high-strung members of the audience. Couldn't we rig up a speaker of some sort for the voice to come out of?"

"Hmmm . . ." Case strode up and down, puffing at his cigar. Chester fidgeted in his chair. Fifty feet away the iguanodon moved from the shelter of a great maple into the open. There was a rending of branches as the heavy salamander head pulled at a mass of foliage thirty feet above the forest floor.

"I've got it!" Case said, smacking his fist into his palm. "Another great idea! You said something about fixing up a speaker for the voice to come out of. But what kind of speaker, Chester?"

"Keep it down." Chester moved behind his chair, a nervous eye on the iguanodon. "I still think that monster can hear us."

"So what? Now, the speaker ought to be mobile—you know, so it can travel around the marks and answer their questions. So . . . we get the computer to rig us a speaker that matches the voice!''

"Look," said Chester, "it's starting to turn this way."

"Pay attention, Chester. We get the machine to design us a robot in the shape of a good-looking dame. She'll be a sensation: a gorgeous, stacked babe who'll answer any question you want to ask her."

"He seems to move very sluggishly," said Chester.

"We could call this babe Miss I-Cutie."

"He sees us."

"Don't you get it? I.Q.—I-Cutie."

"Yes, certainly. Go right ahead; whatever you say."

The iguanodon's great head swung ponderously, stopped with one unwinking eye fixed dead on Chester. "Just like a bird watching a worm," he quavered. "Stand still, Case; maybe he'll lose interest."

"Nuts." Case stepped forward. "Who's scared of a picture?" He stood, hands on hips, looking at the towering reptile. "Not a bad illusion at all," he called. "Even right up close, it looks real. Even smells real." He wrinkled his nose, came stamping back to the two chairs and Chester. "Relax, Chester. You look as nervous as a bank teller at the fifty-credit window."

Chester looked from Case to the browsing saurian. "Case, if I didn't know there was a wall there . . ."

"Hey, look over there." Case waved his cigar. Chester turned. With a rustling of leaves a seven-

43

foot bipedal reptile stalked into view, tiny forearms curled against its chest. In dead silence it stood immobile as a statue, except for the palpitation of its greenish-white throat. For a long moment it stared at the two men. Abruptly, it turned at a tiny sound from the grass at its feet and pounced. There was a strangled squeal, a flurry of motion. The eighteen-inch head came up, jaws working, to resume its appraisal of Chester and Case.

"That's good material," Case said, puffing hard at his cigar. "Nature in the raw; the battle for survival. The customers will eat it up."

"Speaking of eating, I don't like the way the thing's looking at me."

The dinosaur cocked its head, took a step closer.

"Phewww!" Case said. "You can sure smell that fellow." He raised his voice. "Tone it down a little, Computer. This kid has got halitosis on a giant scale."

The meat-eater gulped hard, twice, flicked a slender red tongue between rows of needlelike teeth in the snow-white cavern of its mouth, took another step toward Chester. It stood near the edge of the rug now, poised, alert, staring with one eye. It twisted its head, brought the other eye to bear.

"As I remember, there was at least six feet of clear floor space between the edge of that rug and the wall," Chester said hoarsely. "Case, that hamburger machine's in the room with us!"

Case laughed. "Forget it, Chester. It's just the effect of the perspective or something." He took a step toward the allosaurus. Its lower jaw dropped.

The multiple rows of white teeth gleamed. Saliva gushed, spilled over the scaled edge of the lipless mouth. The red eye seemed to blaze up. A great clawed bird-foot came up, poised over the rug.

"Computer!" Chester shouted. "Get us out of here!"

The forest scene whooshed out of existence.

Case looked at Chester disgustedly. "What'd you want to do that for? I wasn't through looking at them."

Chester took out a handkerchief, sank into a chair, mopped at his face. "I'll argue the point later—after I get my pulse under control."

"Well, how about it? Was it great? Talk about stark realism!"

"Realism is right! It was as though we were actually there, in the presence of that voracious predator, unprotected!"

Case sat staring at Chester. "Hold it! You just said something, my boy: 'as though we were actually there . . .'"

"Yes, and the sensation was far from pleasant."

"Chester"—Case rubbed his hands together—"your troubles are over. It just hit me: the greatest idea of the century. You don't think the tax boys will buy a slice of show biz, hey? But what about the scientific marvel of the age? They'll go for that, won't they?"

"But they already know about the computer."

"We won't talk to 'em about the computer, Chester. They wouldn't believe it anyway; Crmblznski's Limit, remember? We'll go the truth one better. We'll tell 'em something that will knock 'em for a loop."

"Very well, I'll ask: What will we tell them?"

"We tell 'em we've got a real, live time machine!"

"Why not tell them we're in touch with the spirit world?"

Case considered. "Nope, too routine. There's half a dozen in the racket in this state alone. But who do you know that's got a time machine working, eh? Nobody, that's who! Chester, it's a gold mine. After we pay off the Internal Revenue boys, we'll go on to bigger things. The possibilities are endless."

"Yes, I've been thinking about a few of them: fines for tax evasion and fraud, prison terms for conspiracy and perjury. Why not simply tell the computer to float a loan?"

"Listen, up to now you're as clean as a hired man catching the last bus back from the fair. But once you start instructing the machine to defraud by mail for you, you're on the spot. Now keep cool and let's do this as legal as possible."

"Your lines of distinction between types of fraud escape me."

"We'll be doing a public service, Chester. We'll bring a little glamour into a lot of dull, drab lives. We'll be public benefactors, sort of. Why not look at it that way?"

"Restrain yourself, Case. We're not going into politics; we're just honest, straightforward charlatans, remember?"

"Not that there won't be problems," Case went on. "It's going to be a headache picking the right kind of scenes. Take ancient Greece, for example. They had some customs that wouldn't do for a family-type show. In the original Olympics none of the contestants wanted to be loaded with anything as confining as a G string. And there were the public baths—coeducational—and the slave markets, with the merchandise in full view. We'll have to watch our step, Chester. Practically everything in ancient history was too dirty for the public to look at.''

''We'd better restrict ourselves to later times when people were Christians,'' Chester said. ''We can show the Inquisition, seventeenth-century witch burnings—you know, wholesome stuff.''

''How about another trial run, Chester? Just a quickie. Something simple, just to see if the machine gets the idea.''

Chester sighed. ''We may as well.''

''What do you say to a nice cave-man scene, Chester?'' said Case. ''Stone axes, animal skins around the waist, bear-tooth necklaces—the regular Alley Oop routine.''

''Very well—but let's avoid any large carnivores. They're overly realistic.''

There was a faint sound from behind them. Chester turned. A young girl stood on the rug, looking around as if fascinated by the neo-Victorian décor. Glossy dark hair curled about her oval face. She caught Chester's eye and stepped around to stand before him on the rug, a slender, modest figure wearing a golden suntan and a scarlet hair ribbon. Chester gulped audibly. Case dropped his cigar.

''Perhaps I should have mentioned, Mr. Chester,'' the computer said, ''that the mobile speaker you requested is ready. I carried on the work in an entropic vacuole, permitting myself thereby to produce a complex entity in a very brief period, subjectively speaking.''

Chester gulped again.

''Hi!'' Case said, breaking the stunned silence.

''Hello,'' said the girl. Her voice was melodiously soft. She reached up to adjust her hair ribbon, smiling at Case and Chester. ''My name is Genie.''

''Uh . . . wouldn't you like to borrow my shirt?''

''Knock it off, Chester,'' Case said. ''You remind me of those characters you see on Tri-D that hide every time they see a pretty girl in the bathtub.''

''I don't think the computer got the idea after all,'' Chester said weakly.

''It's pretty literal,'' Case said. ''We only worried about the scenes . . .''

''I selected this costume as appropriate to the primitive setting,'' the girl said. ''As for my physical characteristics, the intention was to produce the ideal of the average young female, without mammary hypertrophy or other exaggeration, to evoke a sisterly or maternal response in women, while the reaction of male members of the audience should be a fatherly one.''

''I'm not sure it's working on me,'' said Chester, breathing hard.

The pretty face looked troubled. ''Perhaps the body should be redesigned, Mr. Chester.''

''Don't change a thing,'' Case said hastily. ''And call me Case.''

Chester moved closer to Case. ''Funny,'' he whispered. ''She talks just like the computer.''

''What's funny about that? It *is* the computer

talking. This is just a robot, remember, Chester."

"Shall we proceed with the view of Neolithic Man?" Genie inquired.

"Sure, shoot," Case boomed.

The walls seemed to fade from view to reveal a misty-morning scene of sloping grassland scattered with wild flowers and set here and there with trees.

"Say, this is O.K.," said Case, lighting a fresh cigar. "Nice-looking country."

Case and Chester turned.

Two squat, bearded men in fur pants emerged from a thicket down the slope, saw the watching trio and stopped dead. More savages followed. The two leaders stood, eyes and mouths agape, hefting long sticks sharpened at one end.

"These guys are practically midgets," Case said. "I thought cave men were pretty big guys."

"They seem to see us," said Chester. "Apparently the audience is on view as well as the actors. I feel rather exposed. What do you suppose they're planning to do with those spears?"

One of the natives stepped forward a pace and shouted.

"You too, pal," Case called, puffing out smoke.

The spokesman shouted again, pointing around, at the other man, at the trees, at the sky, then at himself. Bearded warriors continued to appear from the underbrush.

"I wonder what he's yelling about," said Case.

"He says that he is the owner of the world and that you have no business in it," Genie replied.

"His title to the property is probably clearer than mine," put in Chester.

"How the heck do you know the language?" Case asked admiringly.

"Oh, I have full access to the memory banks," Genie said, "as long as I remain within the resonance field."

"Sort of a transmitter and receiver arrangement?"

"In a sense. Actually it is more analogous to an artificially induced telepathic effect."

"I thought that was only with people—uh, I mean, you know, regular-type people."

"Regular in what way?" Genie inquired interestedly.

"Well, after all, you *are* a machine," said Case. "Not that I've got anything against machinery."

"The owner of the world is coming this way," interrupted Chester. "And reinforcements are still arriving."

"Yeah, we're drawing a good crowd," Case said.

The troglodytes spread out in a wide half-circle. The leader called instructions, made complicated motions, turned to hurl an occasional imprecation at the three viewers on the slope.

"Looks like he's getting some kind of show ready. Probably a quaint native dance to get on our good side."

"He's disposing the warriors for battle," Genie said.

"Battle? Who with?" Case looked around. "I don't see any opposition."

"With us. Or, more properly, with you two gentlemen."

"Maybe a strategic withdrawal?" Chester offered.

"I wouldn't miss this for all the two-dollar bills in Tijuana," said Case. "Relax, Chester. It's only a show."

At a signal the half-ring of bearded warriors started up the slope, spears held at the ready.

"Boy, will they get a shock when they hit the wall," Case said, chuckling.

Yelping, the advancing savages broke into a run. They were fifty feet away, thirty . . .

"*I* know they can't get at us," Chester wailed, "but do they?"

"Perhaps I should mention," observed Genie above the din, "that a one-to-one spacio-temporal contiguity has been established."

Genie's voice was drowned out in the mob yell as the warriors pelted up the last few yards, converging on the rug.

At the last instant, Case tossed his cigar aside and leaped up, swung a roundhouse right that sent a hairy warrior spinning. Chester leaped aside from another, saw Case seize two men by their beards and sling their heads together, drop them as three more sprang on him, then go down in an avalanche of whiskers and bandy legs. Chester opened his mouth to shout an order to retreat, got an instant's glimpse of a horny foot aimed at his head. . .

Somewhere, a large brass bell tolled sundown. For a fading moment, Chester was aware of the tumble of dirt-brown bodies, distant cries, an overpowering odor that suggested unsuccessful

51

3

THE SUN WAS SHINING in Chester's eyes. He opened them, felt sharp pains shooting down from the top of his skull, closed them again with a groan. He rolled over, felt the floor sway under him.

"We'll have to cut down on all this drinking," he muttered. "Case, where are you?"

There was no answer. Chester tried his eyes again. If he barely opened them, he decided, it wasn't too bad. And to think that this gargantuan headache had resulted from the consumption of a few bottles of what had always been reputed to be some of the best wines in the old boy's cellar.

"Case?" he croaked, louder this time. He sat up, felt the floor move again sickeningly. He lay back hastily. It hadn't been more than two bottles at the most, or maybe three. He and Case had been looking over the computer . . .

"Oh, no," Chester said aloud. He sat up, winced, pried his eyes open.

He was sitting on the floor of a wicker cage six

feet in diameter, with sides that curved into a beehive shape at the top. Outside the cage, nothing was visible but open air and distant treetops. He pushed his face up against the openwork side, saw the ground swaying twenty feet below.

"Case," he yelled. "Get me out of here!"

"Chester," a soft voice called from nearby. Chester looked around. Twenty feet away, a cage like his own swung from a massive branch of the next tree. Inside it Genie knelt, her face against the rattan bars.

"Genie, where are we?" Chester called. "Where's Case? What's become of the house?"

"Hey!" a more distant voice called. Chester and Genie both turned. Across the clearing, a third cage swayed. Chester made out Case's massive figure inside.

"Couldn't get through the wall, eh?" Chester taunted in a sudden revival of spirit. "Just a show, eh? Of all the idiotic . . ."

"O.K., O.K., a slight miscalculation. But how the heck was I suppose to know Genie was cooking up a deal like that? How about it, Genie? Is that the kind of show you think an audience would go for at two-fifty a head?"

"Don't blame Genie," Chester shouted. "I'm sure she did no more than follow instructions—to the letter."

"We never asked for the real article," Case yelled.

"On the contrary, that's exactly what you demanded."

"Yeah, but how was I to know the damn machine'd take me literally? All I meant was—"

"When dealing with machinery, always specify *exactly* what you want. I should have thought that meat-eating reptile would have been enough warning for you. I told you the infernal creature was in the room with us, but you—"

"But why didn't Genie stop 'em?"

"Should I have?" said Genie. "I had no instructions to interfere with the course of events."

Case groaned. "Let's call a truce, Chester. We've got a situation to deal with here. Afterwards we can argue it out over a couple of bottles of something. Right now we need a knife. You got one?"

Chester fumbled in his pockets, brought out a tiny pen-knife. "Yes, such as it is."

"Toss it over."

"I'm locked in a cage, remember?"

"Oh. Well, get to work and cut the rope."

"Case, I think you must have been hit on the head too—but harder. Have you considered the twenty-foot drop to the ground *if* I could cut the rope, which I can't reach?"

"Well, you got any better ideas? The bird cage is no pushover; I can't bust anything loose."

"Try hitting it with your head."

"Chester, your attitude does you no credit. This is your old pal Case, remember?"

"You're the ex-acrobat. You figure it out."

"That was a few years ago, Chester, and—hey!" Case interrupted himself. "What a couple of dopes! All we got to do is tell Genie to whisk us back home. I don't know what this setup is she got us into, but she can just get us out again. Good ol' Genie. Do your stuff, kid."

"Are you talking to me, Mr. Mulvihill?" Genie asked, wide-eyed.

"Huh? Listen, Genie, this is no time to go dumb! Get us out of this fix! Fast!"

Genie looked thoughtful. "I'm afraid that's beyond my capabilities, Mr. Mulvihill."

Chester gulped hard. "Genie, you brought us here. You've got to get us back!"

"But, Chester, I don't know how."

"You mean you've lost your memory?"

"Oh, no, my memory is excellent."

"What is this, a mechanical mutiny?" Case yelled.

"I think I know what the trouble is," Chester called across to Case. "Genie told us she was linked to the memory banks as long as she remained within the resonance field of the computer. But we must be a considerable distance from the apparatus now—and thus Genie has no contact with the machine."

"Some machinery," Case grumbled.

"As soon as we're back where we left the rug and chairs, I'm sure she'll re-establish contact," Chester said. "Right, Genie?"

"I don't know. But perhaps you're right, Chester."

"This isn't getting us out of here," Case cut in. "Let's cut the chatter and figure what we're going to do. Chester, you can use your knife to cut some of the lashings holding the cage together. Then you can crawl up the rope, make it to my tree, and let me out. Then we cut Genie down, and—"

"Listen!" Chester interrupted. "I hear them coming!"

He peered out at the bright morning-lit clearing below them, the surrounding forest, a trail that wound away between the trees. A group of savages appeared, moving along briskly, filling into the clearing, gathering under the trees. They looked up at the captives, jabbering, pointing and laughing. Two of them set about erecting a wobbly ladder of bamboo-like cane against Case's tree, jabbering as they adjusted it.

"What are they talking about, Genie?" Chester asked. "Or can't you understand them any more?"

Genie nodded. "I absorbed the language when we first arrived."

"In two minutes?"

"Oh, yes. That's one of the advantages of a direct telepathic contact with a data source."

"So you still know everything—except how to get us out of here."

"The actual environmental manipulation was handled by the computer. I was merely the mobile speaker, you recall."

"I guess so," Chester peered down at the natives. "What are they saying?"

"They're discussing a forthcoming athletic event. Apparently a great deal depends upon its outcome."

She listened further as the savages got the ladder in place. One of the bearded men scaled it, fumbled with the end of the rope supporting Case's cage.

"It is to be a contest between champions," said Genie. "A mighty struggled between giants."

"Hey," yelled Case, "if that knee-length Gargantua lets that rope go, I won't be around to watch the bout."

"It's O.K.," Chester called. "There's a sort of pulley-like arrangement of crossbars the rope is wound around. They can't let it down slowly."

Case's cage lurched, dropped a foot, then steadied and moved smoothly down to thump against the ground. The savages gathered around, unlaced and opened a panel in the side, stepped back and stood with leveled spears as Case emerged. He looked around, made a grab for the nearest spear. Its owner danced back. The other shouted, laughed and jabbered excitedly.

"What's all the chatter about, Genie?" Case called.

"They are admiring your spirit, size and quickness of movement, Mr. Mulvihill."

"They are, huh? I'll show 'em some quickness of movement if one of 'em 'll get close enough for me to grab him."

Chester looked up at a sound from across the clearing. A second group of natives was approaching—and in their midst, towering over them, came a hulking brute of a man, broad, thick, hairy.

"Looks like they went for their big brother," Case said. "Quite a guy. He's got muscles like a waterfront bartender."

"This is one of the champions who will engage in combat," said Genie. "Their name for him seems to be translatable as 'Biter-off of Heads.'"

Case whistled. "Look at those hands—as big as a Chinaman's briefcase. He could squeeze one of these midgets like a tube of toothpaste."

"This should be an interesting battle," said Chester, "if his opponent is anywhere near his size."

"I'll lay you three to two on this boy without seeing the challenger," Case called. "I hope they let us hang around and watch."

"Oh, there's no doubt that you'll be present, Mr. Mulvihill," Genie said reassuringly. "You're the one who's going to fight him."

"Chester, it's the best we can do," said Case. "We haven't got much time left to talk. The main bout's coming up any minute now."

"But, Case, against that man-eater you don't have a chance."

"I used to fill in for the strong man on Wednesday afternoons, Chester. And I'll bet you a half interest in Great-grandpop's booze supply that this kid never studied boxing or judo—and I did. Leave that part to me. You do what I told you."

Half a dozen jabbering, gesticulating natives closed in around Case, indicated with jabs of their hardwood spears that he was to move off in the direction of the hairy champion.

"Poor Mr. Mulvihill," Genie said. "That brute is even larger than he is."

"Case knows a few tricks, Genie. Don't worry about him."

The two watched anxiously as the crowd formed up a circle about the local heavyweight and Case. One of the savages shouted for attention, then launched into a speech. The shaggy giant—all of seven feet tall—eyed Case, scowled, stopped to scratch, became absorbed in the pursuit of a louse, began to rotate like a dog chasing its tail, with one arm raised and the other halfway round his back.

"He doesn't look very bright," Chester said. "But what a reach! He's got hold of his own backbone!"

"I hope Mr. Mulvihill is noting the primitive's weaknesses and planning his strategy accordingly."

A dozen yards from his opponent Case stood drawing deep breaths and letting them out slowly. He glanced up, caught Chester's eye, and winked. The speech-maker jabbered on.

"He's telling the people that Mr. Mulvihill is a demon which he summoned from the underworld," Genie said. "He refers to you as the Demon with Four Eyes and to me as the Naked Goddess. Mr. Mulvihill is under some sort of spell which will force him to fight fiercely against the large savage."

"Oh-oh," Chester cut in. "Here we go."

The native leader had stopped speaking. The crowd fell silent. Case pulled off his leather belt and wrapped it around his fist. The hairy seven-footer growled, eying the crowd, stalked forward, still slapping his chest. He stopped, turned his back to Case, and roared out a string of gibberish. Case took three rapid steps, slammed a vicious right to the kidneys.

"Go get him, Case!" Chester yelled.

The giant whirled with a bellow, reaching for the injured spot with a huge right hand and for Case with the left. Case ducked, drove a left to the pit of the shaggy stomach, followed with a right—and went flying as the giant caught him with an openhanded swipe. Case rolled, came to his feet.

The native champion had both hands to his stomach now; his hoarse breathing was audible to Chester, forty feet away.

"Case hurt him that time."

"But Mr. Mulvihill—perhaps he's injured too!"

"I don't think so. His profanity sounds normal. In any event he has their attention fully occupied. I'd better get started."

Chester took out the penknife, looked over the lacing that secured the woven bamboo strips and started sawing.

"I hope this blade holds out. I never contemplated cutting anything more resistant than a cigar tip when I bought it."

"Please work quickly, Chester. Mr. Mulvihill may not last long."

Below, Case ducked aside from a charge, planted a hearty right in the big man's short ribs, danced back as the other changed direction.

"There's one," said Chester as the strands of lacing fell free. "I think three more may do it. Anyone looking my way?"

"No, no one. Ohhh, Chester, I'm frightened. Mr. Mulvihill tripped and barely rolled aside in time to avoid being trampled."

"Hey, don't revert to the feminine now, Genie. Keep the computer aspect of your personality to the fore; it has a steadying effect."

"Mr. Mulvihill has just struck the savage a very effective blow on the back of the neck," said Genie. "It staggered him."

"Two loose. I hope Case has a few more unorthodox blows in his repertoire. I'll need at least ten minutes . . ."

Chester worked steadily, freed a third joint, pulled a vertical member aside, and thrust his head through the opening. It was a close fit, but a moment later his shoulders were through. He reached up for a handhold, pulled himself entirely through, and clung to the wicker frame of the cage. He found a foothold, clambered higher, reached the rope from which the basket was suspended. A glance toward the fighters showed that all eyes were on the combatants. Chester took a deep breath, started up the rope.

The crowd shouted as Case hammered a left and a right to the giant's body, turned to duck away, slipped, and was folded into his opponent's immense embrace.

"Chester, he'll be crushed," wailed Genie.

Chester hung on, craning to see. Case struggled, reached behind him, found an index finger and twisted. The giant roared; Case bent the finger back, back . . .

With a howl the giant dropped him, twisting his hand free, and popped the injured member into his mouth.

Chester let out a long breath, pulled himself up onto the branch to which the rope was secured. He rose shakily to his feet, made his way to the main truck, climbed up to the branch from which Genie's cage was suspended, started out along it. In the clearing below, the crowd yelled. Chester caught a glimpse of Case darting past the giant, whirling to chop hard at the side of his neck with the edge of his hand.

Then Chester was at the rope, sliding down.

"Chester, you'd better leave me. Save yourself."

Chester sawed at the bindings of Genie's cage. "Even if I were enough of a coward to entertain the notion, it would hardly be a practical idea. Just another minute or two, Genie."

The joints parted. Below, Case battled on. Chester pried the rattan aside, held the bars apart as Genie slipped through. She climbed up, reached the rope, shinnied up it easily. Chester followed.

Above him Genie gasped and pointed. Chester turned in time to see Case duck under a mighty haymaker, come up under his huge opponent and spill him off his feet. As the lumbering savage struggled up with a roar, Case caught him on the point of the jaw with a tremendous clout, knocking him flat again. The bigger man shook his head, stumbled to his feet and charged. Case threw himself against the oncoming behemoth's knees. Chester winced as the immense figure dived headlong over Case's crouched figure and smashed into the packed earth, face first. When the dust settled Case was on his feet, breathing hard; the giant lay like a felled tree.

"Unfortunate timing," muttered Chester. "He should have held their attention for another five minutes."

"They're sure to notice us now," Genie whispered, flattening her slender length against the rough bark.

"Don't move," Chester breathed. "We'll wait and see what happens next."

The crowd, standing mute with astonishment,

suddenly whooped, surged in to clap Case on the back, prod the fallen champion, dance about jabbering excitedly. Chester saw Case shoot a quick glance toward the cages, then stoop suddenly, come up with two large, smooth stones. The crowd grew still, drawing back. One or two unlimbered spears. Case raised his hand for silence, then casually tossed one of the stones up, transferred the other to his right hand in time to catch the first with his left, tossed up the second stone. . .

"That's the idea," Chester whipered. "Good old Case. He'll entrance them with his juggling routine. Let's go, Genie."

They clambered silently to the ground. Chester looked back to see Case snatch up a third stone, add it to the act. The natives watched, mouths open. In the shelter of a giant tree bole Chester and Genie paused for an instant, then stole away from the clearing, found a rough trail among the trees, broke into a run. Behind them the cheers of the savages rose, growing fainter now, fading in the distance.

"In the clear," Chester gasped, pulling level with Genie. "Now all we have to do is search a few hundred square miles of woods until we find the rug and the chairs."

"That's all right, Chester," said Genie, running lightly at his side. "I think I know the way."

"Well," Chester puffed, "let's just hope that when we get there the computer is still waiting with its meter ticking."

4

CHESTER STAGGERED the last few yards across the grassy slope to the rug and sank down in one of the yellow chairs. "Next time I go for a romp in the woods," he said, groaning, "I'm going to be wearing a good grade of boots; these melon-slicers are killing me."

"I see no signs of pursuit," said Genie. "Mr. Mulvihill is apparently still holding their attention successfully."

"Hold it, Genie." Chester pointed. "There's smoke rising from back there. You don't suppose . . . ?"

Genie looked concerned. "I don't think they've had time to start roasting Mr. Mulvihill—yet."

"Good Lord, Genie. You think—maybe. . . ?"

"It isn't impossible, judging from what I observed of the cultural pattern."

Chester got to his feet. "We have to go back, Genie. Maybe we can surprise them."

"As you wish, Chester. But I'm afraid we would accomplish nothing. Neither of us is sufficiently robust to overcome an antagonist by force."

Chester's shoulders slumped. "I've always led such a . . . civilized life. I never thought I'd have any occasion for muscles."

"We'd better go on, Chester. We'll obtain arms and hurry back."

"I suppose that's all we can do. Poor Case—he's probably broiling alive. He sacrificed himself for us. For heaven's sake, hurry. Genie! You *are* in contact, I hope?"

Genie considered, then smiled doubtfully. "Yes, I think so. I'll try. Stand close to me, Chester."

He gripped her hand. The sunny scene faded, to be replaced by a wide expanse of black macadam: a city street. All around, tall buildings struck upward out of shadow into high sunlight. A rumbling machine swerved past on the left. Two smaller ones, snorting, veered by on the right in a bowl of brakes. An immense truck bore down, air brakes hissing, ground to a halt, towering over the brocaded chairs with its front tires resting on the fringed edge of the rug. Behind the dusty windshield, the driver yelled and shook his fist. The shout was drowned in a torrent of horns, voices, engines. Chester leaped up for the sidewalk, pulling Genie with him.

"Something's wrong!" he gasped. "Where are we, Genie?"

"I don't know; there's some sort of imbalance in the co-ordinates, Chester! Maybe it's because Mr. Mulvihill was left behind."

A stout man with an open vest over a soiled shirt discarded a toothpick and stepped from a doorway under three tarnished brass spheres.

"Hey, sister, ain't you forgot something?" He leered as he lowered his eyes to ankle level and came up slowly. A man behind him jostled him aside.

"Hiya, babe," he said breezily." A broad like you and me could get along, kiddo. You're kinda skinny, but Benny likes 'em thataway."

Chester stepped forward. "You don't understand. We're involved in experimental . . ." Benny glanced at him, rammed stiff fingers into his sternum. "Get lost, punk." Chester doubled over, gasping. The crowd ringing the tableau separated as a wide figure in a pink uniform and a chrome-plated helmet pushed through, nightstick twirling. He looked Genie over, reached for her arm.

"Come on, sister, I'm takin' you in."

Genie swung a full-handed slap that sent the gaudily dressed cop staggering back. "Chester, let's run!" She seized his hand; he straightened painfully, scrambled after her. The crowd parted again, gaping.

"Give it to 'em, kiddo," a drunk called cheerfully. The cop lunged, tripped over the drunk's outstretched foot, hit with a crunch.

A narrow alleyway opened ahead; Chester and Genie sprinted down it, rounded a corner, dodged garbage cans, emerged into a sheltered court hung with faded washing.

"I don't hear anyone chasing us," Chester gasped. "I don't know where you've landed us, Genie, but we're a long way from home. It looks like a parody of a twentieth-century scene—except for that pink policeman."

"I don't understand it, Chester," Genie wailed. "I was sure I used the proper angle of *pi* over *rho* squared . . ."

"The mob acted normal enough. Lucky they're spectator sports." Chester plucked a long-armed shirt from the lowest line, draped about Genie's shoulders. "I've got to get you some clothes. Duck into a doorway and look inconspicuous. I'll be back as soon as I can."

Ten minutes later, Chester returned, arms laden. "I found a sporting-goods store," he panted. "This is a strange place you've brought us to, Genie. I had to open something called a charge account."

Genie wriggled into a pair of nylon panties, size 5, a 34B brassiere, a pair of whipcord riding breeches, a white linen shirt, a green tweed hacking jacket, and a pair of low-cut riding boots.

"You look charming, Genie," Chester commented. "Like a picture in an old book. Now we can—"

"Oh dear, someone's coming!" Genie exclaimed. "Shall we hide?"

"You take the doorway; I'll get back of the garbage bin!" Chester dived for shelter as a cop with a bruised eye appeared at the alley mouth.

"There she is, boys!" he called. "I told youse . . ."

Chester peered from hiding, saw a half a dozen cops fan out.

"Watch her, boys. She's some kind of wild dame from the circus. Now, sister, are you going to come along peaceable?"

"Hey, Sarge, I thought you said she was nood."

"So now she's got clothes on. It's the same broad."

The cops approached warily. "She don't look tough to me," a fat cop stated. From shelter, Chester thrust out a foot. The cop, moving in briskly for the pinch, hooked an ankle, leaped face first into a patch of spilled garbage. The others charged as Genie darted from the doorway. Hoarse yells rang; cops struggled. Chester sprang to the rescue, put a foot in the garbage slick . . .

A shower of fire shimmered, fading into darkness.

Chester's head ached. He turned over, snuggled down to go back to sleep. He'd have to complain to the management about the mattress; and he was cold, too. He groped for a blanket, felt a rough wall, opened one eye and stared at iron bars and concrete. He sat up, fingering a large knot at the back of his head.

"Genie?" he called hopefully. There was no answer. He rose and went to the door. With his face against the bars, Chester peered along the corridor. The other cells in view were empty. Twenty feet distant, an unshaven man in blue overalls over tattletale-gray longjohns dozed at a desk under a bare sixty-watt light bulb. There was a curled calendar on the wall behind him, featuring a girl, stripped to a G string, hip boots and a deerstalker cap, holding a BB gun. Chester squinted, made out numerals: 1967. He groaned. Somehow, he thought, Genie had landed them in a grotesque parody of the simple halcyon days of a century before, when life had been leisurely and colorful. Chester called again, softly. Somewhere water dripped. There were faint street noises.

He went back to the gray-blanketed bunk, wincing at the throbbing in his head, and sorted through the objects in the seal-away pockets of his sports jacket. Apparently the local cops hadn't managed to find them:

A permatch in a silver case.

A plastic credit card, showing a balance of twenty-one credits.

A half-used packet of Chanel dope sticks.

A buttonhole Tri-D pickup, with attached contact screens.

Not much there, Chester reflected sadly, that would be of help in forcing the steel door of the primitive cell. He twiddled the control of the Tri-D idly, winced at the sudden boom of cacophony, turned the volume low.

"Well, Jim," a tiny voice said. "Here we are in a spaceship, on our way to Venus."

"Yes, Bob," an even tinier voice replied. "We barely escaped capture by the corrupt Space Patrol, which fears we will reveal what we've learned of their illegal operations."

"Yes, Jim. However, if we can only reach the safety of Venus ahead of them, we can enlist the help of Professor Zorch, famed for his researches into abstruse scientific matters, and like that . . ."

Chester flipped the set off. Canned entertainment hadn't changed. On Tri-D, people were always able to adapt ball-point pens into Mark I blasters and fight their way out of any situation—but what could one do with a high-polymer credit card? Or a dope stick? The Tri-D was no better. As for the permatch . . .

Hmmm. Chester fingered the case, opened it and took out the slender two-inch tube of fused quartz with its cluster of components in a quarter-inch bulb at one end. Hadn't he read somewhere that it was dangerous to tamper with a permatch, since it was easy to throw the delicate lens alignment out of adjustment?

Carefully, Chester pried off the tiny protective cap, exposing the factory-set adjusting screw. Now he needed a tool.

The stiff corner of the credit card served nicely. Chester thumbed the permatch alight, then minutely turned the screw. The flame darted out in a thin blue streamer. He turned it farther; the flame winked out. He stared at it unhappily. A two-inch flame wasn't going to help. A faint acrid odor made Chester snort. Someone was burning dog hair. The odor grew stronger. Across the room, a tiny brown dot appeared on the scaled paint of the wall, grew larger, turning black at the periphery. A lazy coil of smoke ascended. Chester gaped, then flicked off the match; the smoke faded.

Back at the barred door, Chester squinted along the tiny tube, pressed the stud. The man in the chair slept on peacefully. A half-inch spot on the desk near his elbow bubbled, smoked. Chester moved the beam cautiously across until the long hairs over the dreamer's ear curled suddenly. The man's nose twitched. He slapped at his temple, sat up snorting, looked around. Chester jumped back, dived for the bunk, scrambled under it and huddled in deep shadow against the wall. The unshaven face appeared at the door, blinking into the gloom. There was a muttered exclamation, then a clash of keys. The door opened. Chester took aim, focused on the callused heel of a large bare foot. The man yelped and hopped, grabbing for the singed member. Chester leveled his fire on the other. The man danced, staring wildly around, then made for the door.

"A poltergeist!" he shouted. "Hey, Harney!"

Chester wriggled out from concealment, ducked through the open door, and slid into the shelter of a gray-painted wall locker as heavy feet pounded in the hall.

"Don't tell me," the barefoot cop was shouting. "I seen 'em before, plenty times. They got a kind of attraction fer me. This here one is a bad one. First it picked up m' desk, then it started throwin' things, then it give me two hotfoots."

"Hotfeet," someone snarled. "See if he's got a bottle, Lem."

"Looky here," the barefoot one started. "I guess you boys never heard the time I seen the saucer . . ."

"Don't see no bottle."

Three large backs loomed a yard from Chester's concealment. He aimed through a narrow opening between them, focused on a blanket dangling from a bunk in the cell across the corridor. Smoke rose promptly.

"Hey!" one of the cops barked. "They's su'thin in there!" He backed from view. "I'll go fer help!"

Chester listened as the three men competed for position; three sets of footsteps receded along the hall. Chester pocketed the permatch and headed for a side entrance.

Half an hour later, a shabby brown tweed jacket filched from the station covering his modishly cut but conspicuous plastic-appliqué sports jacket, Chester strolled past the stretch of street where he and Genie had first arrived, now obstructed by large wooden signs lettered DETOUR. Police squad cars were parked three deep at the curb. The area around the rug with its two chairs was blocked off by yellow-painted sawhorses hung with red obstruction lights. A crowd of idlers gaped.

"All right, move along," a cop bawled. "The bomb squad is goin' in now. You folks wanta get blown up?"

Chester paused, scanning the crowd for Genie. No luck. She hadn't been in jail—at least not in the part he had had an opportunity to check. Surely if she were free, she would have come here. Not that it would help. No one could get through that police cordon.

Chester tried hard to think. If only Case were here—or Genie. But unless he could get back to the rug, he'd never see either of them again.

Case would be thoroughly roasted by now, of

course, if that *had* been the purpose of the fire he'd seen—but perhaps that was being overly pessimistic. Perhaps Case was still juggling away, casting anxious glances down the jungle path from time to time, waiting for rescue.

And Genie, being grilled under the hot lights by policemen, who, in spite of their pink coats, were cop all the way through . . .

One of the cops seemed to be looking Chester's way. He sauntered on, whistling, stepped into the first doorway he saw, found himself in a shop plastered with SALE notices and crowded with flimsy tables stacked with gaudily colored merchandise among which bored-looking customers milled, picking over the bargains.

Chester tried to think. He couldn't just stand around; in time, the cops would be sure to notice him. Perhaps if he tried a sudden dash for the rug . . .

He glanced through the window. The cops were large and numerous, the sawhorses closely spaced, the squad cars ominously ready. He could never hope to penetrate that barrier by a surprise move alone; he would have to do something to distract attention and then slip through quietly.

"Git outa da way, ya bastid," a corpulent lady with a mustache and runover shoes said conversationally, nudging Chester aside.

"Oh, excuse me, Madam . . ." Chester moved on to the next counter, found himself nervously fingering a stack of clear plastic bags.

"That's the two-quart size," a salesman said to a man on Chester's left.

Chester picked up a bag. It was good, tough stuff.

"Seals with a hot iron," the salesman was saying.

Chester felt in his pocket. Hmm. His credit card was no good here, of course. He'd have to—

A large placard caught his eye: DON'T ASK FOR CREDIT!

"How do I know what you use 'em for?" the clerk was saying. "You want 'em or don't you?"

The customer mumbled. The clerk turned away. Chester slipped a two-inch sheaf of the plastic bags from the counter and under his coat and headed for the door. As he reached it, a hoarse voice called, "Hey, you. The guy with a funny pants!"

Chester hurled himself between two matrons in garish prints with uneven hemlines and set off at a run. Heads turned to stare. A whistle shrilled behind him. He rounded a corner, saw a short flight of steps with an iron rail. He took them four at a time, banged through a massive glass-paneled door into a dim hallway that smelled of stale vegetable oil, fly spray and deodorant. Carpeted stairs rose into a canyon of yellowed wallpaper. Chester went up, whirled through the landing as the door below banged open.

"In here!" someone yelled.

"Take the back. I'll check upstairs!"

The staircase ended three flights up in a narrow hallway leading to a gray window behind limp curtains. Feet were thudding on the stairs. There were three doors with brown porcelain knobs along each side of the hall. Chester jumped to the first on the left. It rattled but held. The second opened and a blat of sound emerged. Chester sprang for the third door, threw it open, whirled and slammed it behind him. In two jumps he was in the bathroom, pulling open a tarnished mirror. He seized a can of shaving cream, blasted a gob into his hand, slapped it across his face, under his chin. In a quick motion, he pulled off the coat, the sports jacket, tossed them aside, grabbed a bladeless safety razor from the cabinet shelf and scraped a swath through the layer of white lather, then dashed for the door and flung it wide.

A cop thundered past, threw a glance at Chester. "Stay inside, buddy," he bawled.

Chester withdrew, closed the door gently, and let out a long breath. "Who says there's no point in watching the Late Late Late Show?" he murmured.

From the windows, Chester looked down on the crowded street. The rug looked pitifully small in the center of the barricade of sawhorses, cops, cars and curious citizens. The distance was, Chester estimated, fifty feet vertically, and an equal distance out from the face of the building. The sounds in the hall had gone away now. He went into the green enameled bathroom, wiped the lather from his face, recovered his shirt from the living-room floor, then checked through the closet shelves, the bedroom and finally the kitchen. He found an electric iron in a cabinet under the sink. The ironing board was propped in a corner. Chester set it up, plugged in the iron, then counted his plastic bags.

Forty-two of them. Still, there was no use starting on the bags unless he could work out the delivery mechanism.

A thorough search of the apartment turned up a ball of stout twine, nails, a hammer, a heavy-duty stapler, several hundred back issues of *Crude*, The Magazine for Male Men, and a small plastic wastebasket. Chester set to work.

Pounding cautiously, he drove two stout nails into the window sill eight inches apart, and a matching pair into the wall across the room at a level four feet higher, then strung heavy twine across between them in two parallel strands. Next he cut the bottom neatly from the wastebasket and nailed the container to the wall above the previously placed nails, with the smaller, cut-out end down. The next two nails went into the right-hand wall, with two more matching them on the opposite side of the room, just under the ceiling. Again he strung cord between the paired spikes.

Chester paused to listen. There was a murmur of sound from the street, the drip of water from the bathroom, the snarl of an engine gunning somewhere. He went to the refrigerator, took out a can of beer, drank half of it and went back to work.

He opened a copy of *Crude*, stared wonderingly at a double-page spread in full color captioned "Udderly Delightful" and fitted the magazine over one of the cables at the window sill so that the string nestled against the spine, at the center of the thin sheaf of pages. He crimped the other edge of the magazine, folded the creased edge over the other line and stapled it in place to form a shallow trough between the two supporting lines.

The next *Crude* was positioned above the first. Working rapidly, Chester extended the chute across the room to terminate directly under the bottomless wastebasket.

He stepped back to survey his work. The center of the trough had a tendency, he noted, to droop, the edges of the magazines coming almost together. He went to the closet, extracted half a dozen wire coat hangers and bent them into shallow U-shaped braces, which he fitted between the lines at three-foot intervals. The trough now formed a smooth curve from the wastebasket to the window sill.

Fifteen minutes' work completed the other leg of the trough, extending from the left-hand wall in a shallow curve to end above the open top of the wastebasket.

There was a three-inch roll of masking tape on the desk; Chester used it to attach extra sheets bearing photographs of shirtless women to the floor of the trough, lapping the joints between magazines.

Back in the kitchen, he finished the beer, then filled a plastic bag with water, used a length of clothesline wire to assist in folding the top edge over evenly, then applied the warm iron, sealing the plastic. He went to the living room, stepped up on a chair and placed the plastic bag of water in the wastebasket. It dropped an inch or two, then wedged tight in the tapered passage. Chester went back to the kitchen, located a pint bottle nearly full of vegetable oil, returned and poured a generous helping around the plastic bag. It eased down, plopped into the trough below, where Chester caught it and set it aside.

He went back to the kitchen and carefully filled and sealed the remaining forty-one bags. Next he used the ice pick to make a hole in each side of the wastebasket, near the bottom, through which he threaded a length of string. He tied a knot at one end, drew it up snug, then looped the other around a large wooden match which nestled against the outside of the wastebasket, holding the string in position, blocking the bottom of the container. He used a chair to reach the top of the upper trough, into which he poured a liberal dollop of vegetable oil, smearing it out well so that the entire surface of the chute was lubricated. He repeated the operation for the steeper lower section.

Chester went back to the kitchen, where the water bags lay like a clutch of limp dinosaur eggs, selected one, and placed it in the upper end of the higher trough. It slid gently down the long chute and dropped into the wastebasket, easing down to rest against the obstructing string. Then he loaded the magazine trough above with the other bags. The forty-one rounds just filled the available space, lying bulging, end to end.

Chester crossed the room and looked out. The police below were striding about with tape measures, standing with folded arms, posing for photographers, and waving back the crowd that seemed about to engulf the tiny arena of official activity. Cautiously, Chester raised the window twelve inches. Oil dribbled from the end of the trough onto the window sill. He went into the bathroom, ducking under the chute, washed up, smoothed his hair, straightened his shirt, donned his jacket, then removed his heavy silver ring and placed it on the medicine-cabinet shelf beside the shaving cream.

He opened the hall door and looked out. All quiet. The box of matches lay on a table by the door. He lighted one, touched it to the match securing the string which blocked the wastebasket, then sprinted for the stairs, leaped down them five at a time, rounded the landing, took the second flight, pounded down to ground level.

Breathing hard, he paused to glance out the street door. The fringes of the crowd were strung out near the corner. He stepped out, strode along quickly, pushed through the spectators to a position from which the third-story windows were visible. The one directly above the center of activity was open. The curtain billowed slightly; the end of the trough was clearly visible.

Nothing happened.

Chester swallowed. It hadn't taken him more than thirty seconds to make the three flights down to the street. Had the match gone out?

Something flashed in the window, glinted in an arc out over the street, dropped. A strangled yell sounded. The crowd simultaneously surged forward and recoiled, as curiosity struggled with discretion. Chester pushed his way through the press as a second almost invisible missile leaped from the window. "It's radioactive!" someone yelled. The mob churned. A woman screamed. Cops appeared, beating a strategic withdrawal from the field of fire. A third bomb flew from the window, splattered against a tall policeman who yelled and sprang for cover. A fourth bag of water soared out, down and exploded.

"A little under a second apart," Chester muttered, weaving between fleeing citizens. "A little too much oil in the wastebasket."

Four cops remained in the rapidly expanding clearing centered on the rug. One drew his pistol and fired into the air. The other three, eyes on the growing blots on the rug, dropped flat. Chester reached open ground, skirted the first rank of squad cars, seeing the flash of another round, then another. The next fell short, splashed off a police car, sent spray high in the air. Two fat women darted from forward positions, screeching and slapping at water droplets. Chester ducked aside, took an elbow in the ribs, stumbled out into the clear.

"Hey!" a shrill voice sounded behind him. "Ain't you the guy . . ."

Chester threw his leg over the sawhorse.

"That's far enough, Buster," the cop bawled. He took a step forward, bringing the gun around as a bag of water took him in the face. He went down backward. Chester scrambled over, took two steps to the rug.

An immense padded mallet slammed against his head. The world rose up and hit him in the face.

Curious, Chester thought dreamily. *I always pictured H-bombs as being noisy.*

Someone was hauling at his arm.

"This is the bastid, I seen him," someone was screeching. Chester shook his head, pulled free from the grip and struggled to his feet. A hatless cop wavered on all fours between Chester and the rug. The fat woman raised a rolled umbrella. "I'm claimin' the reward," she shrieked. A bomb splattered. The cop focused his eyes on Chester and lunged. Chester ducked away, managing a return jab at the fat woman as he bowled her aside, and sprang for the rug. He skidded to a halt midway between the two brocaded chairs, ducked a bag of water and yelled, "Computer, get me out of here—fast!"

5

THE TALL BUILDINGS, the street, the cops, faded, winked out of existence. The sounds died, cut off abruptly. Chester stood in the center of a wide square paved with varicolored cobblestones and lined with small shops and merchants' stalls. Beyond, a green slope dotted with dazzling white villas swept up to a wooded skyline. People in bright colors moved about, examinging tradesmen's wares, stopping in groups to talk, or strolling at ease. Above a silversmith's shop, white curtains fluttered at open windows. The aroma of crisping bacon drifted across the square. In the distance a flute played a lazy melody.

Chester groaned. "Ye gods, where've you brought me this time, Computer?"

"Your instructions were," the computer's voice spoke from mid-air, "simply to—"

"I know. I always seem to phrase things badly. Every time I make a move, I'm worse off than I was. Now I've lost Case, and Genie, too. Where am I this time?"

"According to my instruments, this *should* be the Chester residence."

"You'd better have your wiring checked."

A brass plate set in the paving underfoot, half concealed by the edge of the rug, caught Chester's eye.

The inscription read: "IT WAS ON THIS SPOT THAT THE LEGENDARY KEZ-FATHER, HERO AND TEACHER, TOOK HIS LEAVE OF THE PEOPLE AFTER BRINGING THEM THE GIFT OF WISDOM. THIS MYTH, WHICH DATES BACK TO THE CULTURE . . ."

"Ye gods," Chester muttered. "I've already violated the local shrine." He moved quickly clear of the spot.

Two men in loose togas, one old, one young, stood nearby, looking earnestly past Chester. He cleared his throat and stepped forward. Nothing to do now but brazen it out.

"I white god," he said. "I come, bring magic stick, go bang, all fall down!"

The two men ignored him. "Remarkable!" the older exclaimed, turning to the younger man, in green. "Did you observe this phenomenon, Devant?"

The other, a well-muscled man with clear blue eyes and flashing white teeth, nodded. "Two curious chairs and a rug. I glanced away for a moment and when I turned back—there they were. I find it difficult to reconcile the manifestation with my world-picture. A very interesting problem."

"Possibly my senility is getting the better of me."

The old man glanced at Chester. "Young man, did you observe the arrival of this furniture?"

Chester cleared his throat. "Not exactly, sir; I have been participating in an experiment, and I seem to have lost my bearings. Could you tell me—"

"No," the old man said, shaking his head resignedly. "That would have been too much to hope for. Why are there never any witnesses to these apparently supernatural manifestations?"

"Is it possible," the man in green cut in, "that this could be the probability crisis that Vasawalie has been predicting?"

"It's not supernatural," Chester said. "Merely a misguided piece of mechanical ineptitude. You see, I—"

"Please, young man; no mechanistic platitudes, if you please."

"You don't understand. This is *my* furniture."

The old man held up a hand. "I fear I must insist on my prior claim. I distinctly observed you to approach from—ah, I'm not sure of the direction, but it was well after I had pointed out the anomaly. In fact, I'm sure you were attracted by my cry of surprise. Correct, Devant?"

"I didn't notice just when he came up," Devant said. "But it was at least five or possibly ten minutes after you and I, Norgo."

"Actually, I was here first," Norgo said. "*You* followed by several minutes, Devant."

"Oh, never mind," Chester said. "Can you just tell me the name of this town?"

"I'll get a crew down right away," said Devant. "I want to examine this *in situ*. Molecular scan, fabric distortion, chronometric phase-interference, Psi band—everything.'' He waved a hand at Chester. ''Please step aside; you're obscuring my view.''

''This will be a serious blow to Randomism,'' said Norgo happily.

''What I wanted to ask was,'' Chester pressed on, ''what year is this? I mean, ah, this isn't by any chance the future, is it?''

The old gentleman looked at Chester squarely for the first time. ''Let us define our terms,'' he said, folding his arms. ''Now . . .''

''What I mean is, this scene here—'' Chester waved a hand—''is something my computer invented—just as a harmless sort of joke, you understand. The problem is . . .''

Norgo blinked. ''I shall do a paper,'' he said, ''on pseudorationalization in response to rejection of—''

''You don't seem to understand,'' cut in Chester. ''I'm lost and my friends are relying on me.''

''It will be the sensation of the Congress,'' Norgo droned on, rubbing his hands together. ''Great Source of Facts. What if I should actually derive germane substantive data from this? That will dispose of the Ordainists, once and for all.''

''Blast the Ordainists,'' Chester burst out. ''I'm in serious difficulties. My best friend is being roasted alive, a young woman of my acquaintance is under detention by primitive police, and you—''

''Dear me, a well-developed delusional system,'' said Norgo. ''Doubtless arising from frustration at having been anticipated in detection of the chair phenomenon. This will be most interesting to the Congress.''

"You're the delusion!" Chester shouted. "I'm getting back on my rug; I'll dissolve this whole fantasy back into the computer banks it came out of!"

Norgo sprang forward. "I must ask you not to disturb the artifacts; they may be highly important scientific exhibits."

"They happen to belong to me." Chester turned, rebounded from the broad, muscular chest of Devant. Five more well-developed locals moved into position around him.

"You'll have to move on," the big man said. "Only technicians will be permitted in this area while the specimens are under study."

Norgo tsked. "We simply can't have these distressing exhibitions by frustrated partisans of misguided philosophical splinter groups. I shall propose to the Congress—"

"I've got to get back to my rug!" Chester made a dive for a gap in the ranks, felt iron hands clamp on his arms.

"Hey, Computer!" he yelled. There was no reply. The hands propelled him quickly along to deposit him well outside the growing circle of spectators.

"Any more disturbances," Devant said coldly, "and I'll have you locked up."

"But . . . how long before you'll be finished?"

"Just run along and amuse yourself. We'll have a great deal to do. It may take a while."

Chester gazed listlessly at the swimming pool rippling in the late-afternoon sun. A pretty brunette in a diaper crossed the terrace and offered a frosted glass. Chester shook his head.

"Shall we go for a swim, Chester?"

"No, thanks, Darina."

"Poor Chester. Can't you cheer up?"

"You don't seem to understand." Chester's voice held a plaintive note. "I've been idling here for weeks now while my friends suffer fates I shudder to contemplate. My computer's probably been dismantled. And those idiotic scholars still won't let me near my rug."

Darina made a sympathetic sound. "The rug is a powerful security symbol to you, isn't it, Chester? I remember a blanket—"

"There's nothing secure about it! It's probably nonfunctional now. And at best, I'll just find myself trapped in another of the computer's preposterous settings. But even that would be better than lounging here, completely ineffectual."

"Chester, have you thought of finding work to do?"

"What kind of work? I just want to get away from here. I've tried five times to creep up on my rug under cover of darkness, but that fellow Devant . . ."

"What were you trained in, Chester?"

"Well," said Chester, considering, "I . . . ah . . . majored in liberal arts."

"You mean you paint pictures?"

"No, nothing like that. Business administration."

"I don't think I've heard of that. Is it a game of skill or chance?"

"Both." Chester smiled patiently. "No, in biz

ad we're taught how to manage large commercial enterprises.''

''I see. And after receiving your training you went on to actual management of some such organization?''

''Well, no. Funny, but I couldn't seem to find any big businessmen who were looking for a fresh college graduate to tell them how to run their companies.''

''Perhaps we'd better try something else. What about the arts?''

''I did do a painting once,'' Chester said hesitantly. ''It had numbers thay you compared with a chart and then you matched that up with the little cans of paint and colored in the spaces.''

''I'm not sure there'd be a large call for that type of skill here.''

''Don't disparage it. President Eisenhower—''

''What about handicrafts? We value the manual skills highly here, Chester.''

''Oh, I've done a lot of that. Built a plastic boll weevil only last month. Over two hundred interlocking parts.''

''You made the parts from plastic?''

''No. I bought a kit. But . . .''

''Perhaps in the field of sports?'' Darina suggested.

Chester blushed. ''Well, of course, in school I was a great fan of outdoor activities. I never missed a game the entire four years.''

''Splendid!'' Darina looked interested. ''We'll be happy to receive instruction in any new types of athletic competition of which you're master.''

"Well, I didn't actually *play*, of course. But I was there in the stands, rooting. And I know some of the rules."

"You didn't play?"

"I was on my fraternity's bridge squad," Chester offered.

"How is that played?" asked Darina, brightening. Chester explained. There was an awkward silence.

"Chester, have you ever performed any useful labor?" Darina asked.

"As a matter of fact, I worked one summer in a factory. I was an instrument spot-checker. I made sure the controls that worked the automatic machinery were functioning properly."

"This involved mechanical skills?"

"If anything had gone wrong with the TV scanner that actually did the inspecting, I was on the spot to see that the back-up scanner took over."

"You activated the emergency equipment, in other words?"

"No, it was automatic. But I assure you, the union regarded my job as essential."

"What about hobbies, Chester?"

"Oh, my, yes; I had a stamp collection."

"Hmmm. Perhaps something a little more active?"

"I built model airplanes as a boy. Of course, I gave that up when I was twelve."

"Why?"

"Well, it seemed a trifle immature. All the other lads my age were already learning golf." Chester broke off as a white-haired elder took a table a few yards distant. "Say, there's that old fool who's behind all this." He rose and crossed to the other table.

"Look here, Mr. Norgo, how long is this absurd business going on? I've been here a month now—and I'm no closer to getting back on my rug than I was. You don't seem to understand—"

"Calmly, Chester," Norgo said, signaling a waitress clad in a wet handkerchief. "It is you who fail to understand. Important work is in progress. Meanwhile, just keep yourself amused."

"I'm in no mood to be amused!"

Norgo nodded thoughtfully. "Perhaps you'd like to participate in an experiment?"

"What is it—vivisection?"

Nórgo considered. "I don't think that will be necessary." He hitched his chair around. "Chester, do you know what our most important natural resource is?"

"What has that to do with my problem?"

"Do you know how often a truly superior intellect is born?"

"Not very often. Look, I—"

"Once in four million, five hundred and thirty-three thousand, two hundred and four births. With a world population of half a billion, the present figure, the rules of probablility allow for the presence among us of only one hundred such gifted persons. And do you know what percentage of these superior individuals are fortunate enough to encounter conditions conducive to the full stimulation of their latent abilities?"

"I'd guess about—"

"Not one per cent," Norgo said flatly. "With luck, one individual."

"Very interesting. But to get back to—"

"If we were content," Norgo pressed on, "to allow unrestrictive increase in the population, we might, one could reason, improve this situation. With a ten-fold increase in population the number of superior intellects should increase to a thousand, you say."

"I didn't say, but—"

"Not so! Environmental factors would deteriorate due to overcrowded conditions. The latent geniuses would find less opportunity to evolve their talents."

"That hardly seems—"

"The true function of the mass of the population is the production, by their sheer numbers, of the occasional genius. It is the objective of our educational system to identify and train such talents— and this can only be done by the realization, in each individual, of the maximum potential."

"Why? So they can grow up and talk like you?"

"Now, life is not an engineering project, Chester. It is a work of art."

"And while you're lecturing on art, my friends are—"

"I have long been interested," Norgo went on imperturbably, "in the purely theoretical problem of the reactions of a mature but untrained mind exposed to a full modern education, in concentrated form, after perhaps twenty-five years of indolence, laziness, carelessness, minimal demand. The pressure, of course, would be tremendous. Would the mind or body break under the stress? Believe me, Chester, the results of such an experiment would be of the most profound importance."

"Not to me. I—"

"Now you, Chester, while possessed of a normal potential, are, beyond the simple abilities to talk and feed yourself, plus a few fringe accomplishments such as playing the game you call bridge, totally untrained. Your body is weak, your will untried, your mind unused—"

"Maybe I don't get out a lot."

"All of which makes you an ideal subject—if you wish to volunteer for the experiment."

"I wish to get back to my rug."

Norgo nodded. "Exactly."

Chester's mouth opened. "You mean—why, this is blackmail!"

"Let us simply say that by the time the experiment is concluded, your—ah—rug will have been released by our research groups."

"How long will that be?"

"I shall attempt, Chester, to impart the equivalent of a twenty-year course of development in a single year."

"A year! But . . ."

"I know; you're concerned for your imaginary playmates."

"I told you . . ."

Norgo turned as a laden tray was placed before him. "Let me know your decision, Chester."

"If I do it—you'll let me back on my rug?"

Norgo nodded, sniffing a dish appreciatively.

"Of all the underhanded, unethical, unwarranted piracy I've ever encountered, this is undoubtedly the most unbelievable,'' Chester said bitterly.

Norgo blinked. "You mean you're refusing?"

"When do I start?"

6

CHESTER AND NORGO clambered down from the open cockpits of the heli in which they had flown out from the Center. Chester looked around at the sweep of meadow, the wooded hills, and a low white building that covered a quarter acre near the crest of the slope. Cut in the white stone above the entry were the words: IS NOT IS NOT NOT IS

Norgo led the way across the grass and into an airy hall where mosaics stood out in brilliant color against white walls.

"Ah, here's Kuve now," Norgo said.

A tall young man with pale blond hair and a square jaw approached through an open archway. He greeted Norgo, studied Chester appraisingly.

"So this is to be my subject," he said, circling Chester. "Remove your shirt, please."

"Right now? I thought I'd have time to unpack, take a shower, stroll around, look over the campus, and then maybe have coffee, get acquainted with the other students, discuss the curriculum, plan a schedule . . ."

Kuve broke in. "There will be no opportunity for coffee or strolls. Your schedule had been planned in advance. You will become acquainted with the plant as necessary."

Chester slowly pulled off his shirt. "It sounds like a strange sort of school. How often will I be able to get back to town?"

"The trousers, please," Kuve said.

"Right here in the lobby?"

Kuve looked at him, surprised. "It is comfortably warm, is it not?"

"Sure, but—"

"Tell me," Kuve said interestedly, "are you under the impression that you are in some way unique?"

"I'm perfectly normal!"

Kuve looked Chester over carefully. "You're going to make a fascinating project," he said approvingly. "Norgo wasn't exaggerating. Almost complete atrophy of the musculature, obvious limited articulation, minimal lung capacity, poor skin tone, barely sub-parthenogenic posture . . ."

"Well, I'm sorry if I don't come up to your expectations."

"Oh, you do indeed. You even exceed them. But don't be concerned. I've worked out a complete developmental scheme for you."

"That's fast work. It hasn't been three hours since I volunteered."

"Oh, I started on it a month ago, when Norgo told me you'd be volunteering."

Chester trailed Kuve along a wide corridor to a

small room lined with wall cabinets. Kuve pointed to one. "You will find garments there. Please put them on."

Chester squeezed into a pair of trunks, laced on sandals, and stood. "Is this all I get? I feel like the New Year."

A shapely young woman in a white kilt entered the room. She smiled at Chester, took a case of instruments from a cabinet, and reached for his hand. "I'm Mina. I'm going to trim your nails back and apply a growth-retarding agent," she said cheerfully. "Hold still now."

"What's this for?"

"Excessively long hair and nails would be a painful nuisance in some of the training," said Kuve. "Now, Chester, I want to ask you something: What is pain?"

"It's . . . umm . . . a feeling that comes from damage to the body."

"Nearly right, Chester. Pain is based on *fear* of damage to the body."

Kuve went to a wall shelf, brought back a small metal article and held it up.

"This is a manual shaving device, once in daily use. This sharp-edged blade was drawn over the skin of the face, cutting the hairs."

"I'm glad I live in modern times."

"Under optimum conditions, the process of removing a single day's growth of facial hair with this instrument occasioned a pain level of .2 agons. Under merely average conditions, however, the level quickly rose to .5 agons, roughly equal to the sensation produced by a second-degree burn."

THE GREAT TIME MACHINE HOAX

"It's amazing what people will put up with," Chester said.

"Are your feet perfectly comfortable, Chester?"

"Certainly. Why shouldn't they be?"

"You have callus tissue on both feet, as well as deformities caused by constricting footwear."

"Well, melon-slicers may not be the most—"

"In order to have produced these conditions, you must have endured pain on the order of .5 agons continuously, for months and years. Yet probably you seldom noticed it."

"Why notice it? There was nothing I could do about it."

"Exactly. Pain is not an absolute; it is a state of mind, which you can learn to disregard."

Kuve reached out, pinched the skin on Chester's thigh. "You can see that I'm merely pressing with very moderate force. You are in no danger of injury."

"Is that a promise?" said Chester nervously.

"Now close your eyes. Concentrate on the sensation of undergoing an amputation of the leg—without anesthetic. The knife slicing through the flesh, the saw attacking the living bone . . ."

Chester squirmed in the chair. "Hey, that hurts! You're bearing down too hard!"

Kuve released his grip. "I squeezed no harder, Chester. The association of the idea of injury intensified the sensation. You paid no attention whatever to Mina when she applied a measured stimulus of .4 agons to the exposed cuticle of your finger while I held your attention. You accepted the twinges of a manicure as normal and non-injurious.''

Chester rubbed his thigh. ''The leg still hurts, I'll have a bruise tomorrow.''

''You may.'' Kuve nodded. ''The control of the mind over bodily functions is extensive.''

Mina finished, flashed a smile at Chester and left the room.

''Let's move along to the gymnasium.'' Kuve led the way along a corridor to a large room, high-ceilinged and fitted with gymnastic equipment. He turned to Chester. ''What is fear?''

''It's . . . uh . . . the feeling you get when you're in danger.''

''It is the feeling that arises when you are unsure of your own capability to meet a situation.''

''You're wrong on that one, Kuve. If a Bengal tiger walked in here I'd be scared, even if I knew exactly how incapable I was.''

''Look around you; what would you actually do if a wild beast did in fact enter this room?''

''Well, I'd run.''

''Where?''

Chester studied the room. ''It wouldn't do any good to start off down the hall; there's no door to stop whatever was chasing me. I think I'd take that rope there.'' He pointed to a knotted fifty-foot cable suspended from among high rafters.

''An excellent decision.''

''But I doubt if I could climb it.''

''So you are unsure of your capabilities.'' Kuve smiled. ''But try, Chester.''

Chester went to the rope, looked at it doubtfully. Kuve muttered into a wrist communicator. Chester grasped the rope, wrapped his legs around it, wriggled up six feet.

"This is . . . the best I can . . . do," Chester puffed. He slid back to the floor.

There was a sound like water gurgling down a drain. Chester turned quickly. An immense tan mountain lion paced toward him, yellow eyes alight, a growl rumbling from its throat. With a yell Chester leaped for the rope, swarmed halfway to the distant rafters, and clung, looking down. Kuve patted the sleek head of the animal; it yawned, nuzzling his leg affectionately.

"You see? You were capable of more than you imagined," Kuve called matter-of-factly.

"Where did that thing come from?" Chester called.

"He's a harmless pet. When you mentioned a tiger, I couldn't resist the opportunity to make an object lesson."

Chester slid down the rope slowly, eyes on the cat. Back on the floor, he edged behind Kuve, who slapped the animal's flank. The animal padded away.

"If I called him back, you wouldn't panic now, because you know he's harmless. And if a really wild animal were released here, you'd know what to do—and that you were capable of doing it. You could watch the Bengal tiger you mentioned quite calmly and take to the rope only if necessary."

"Maybe—but don't try me. That cost me some skin."

"Did you notice that—at the time?"

"All I was thinking about was that man-eater."

"The fear and pain reactions are useful to the unthinking organism. But you have a reasoning mind, Chester. You could dispense with the automatic-response syndromes."

"It's better to be a live coward—"

"But you might be a dead coward, when mastery of fear could have saved you. Look down, Chester."

Chester glanced at the floor. As he watched, the milky white surface cleared to transparency, all but a narrow ribbon on which he stood, scarcely four inches wide, spanning a yawning abyss below his feet set with jagged black rocks. Kuve stood by unconcernedly, apparently suspended in mid-air.

"It's quite all right, Chester. Merely a floor of very low reflectivity."

Chester teetered on the narrow strip. "Get me out of here," he choked.

"Close your eyes," Kuve said quietly. Chester squeezed his eyes shut.

"Forget what you saw," Kuve ordered. "Concentrate on sensing the floor through your feet. Accept its solidity."

Chester swallowed, then opened his eyes slowly. He looked at Kuve. "I guess it will hold," he said shakily.

Kuve nodded. "Working here for a few weeks will help dissipate your irrational fear of heights."

"When weather permits," said Kuve, "you'll do your workouts here on the terrace in the open air."

Chester surveyed the hundred-foot-square area,

floored with dark wood and surrounded by a five-foot wall of flowering shrubs. A cluster of tall poplars shaded a portion of the floor from the high morning sun. Racked against the low wall was an array of weights, bars and apparatus.

"Perhaps I should explain that I have no aspirations to the Mr. Universe title," Chester said. "I think perhaps a couple of Indian clubs would be more than adequate for me."

"Chester," said Kuve, motioning his pupil to a padded bench. "I've taken the first steps toward dispelling your certainty that pain is unendurable and that fear is both useful and overmastering. Now let us consider the role of boredom as a hindrance to the control of the intellect over the body. What is boredom, Chester?"

"Well, boredom sets in when you have nothing to occupy your mind."

"Or when instinct says, 'the activity at hand is not vital to my survival.' It is a more potent factor in influencing human behavior than either fear or pain." He handed Chester a small dumbbell. "Do you find that heavy?"

Chester weighed the five-pound weight in his hand. "No, not really."

"Have another." Chester hefted a dumbbell in each hand. "Now," said Kuve, "please stand and place the two weights at shoulder height. Then press them alternately to arm's length."

Chester thrust the weights up, puffing. A minute passed. His pace grew slower.

Kuve seated himself comfortably in a canvas chair. "You'd like to stop now, Chester. Why?"

"Because . . . I'm getting exhausted . . ." Chester gasped.

"Exhaustion would result in your failure to press the weight up, but it fails to explain the mere desire to stop while strength remains."

"I think I've injured myself," Chester gasped. "I've overexerted."

"No," said Kuve, "you're bored. Therefore you feel the impulse to stop—nature's automism for conserving energy vital to the hunt, flight, combat, or mating. From now on I'll expect you to reject its control of your motivations."

It was late afternoon. Chester let his hand fall from the hand grip of the machine which he had been squeezing, twisting, pulling and pushing at Kuve's direction. He groaned.

"I thought you were exaggerating when you said you were going to test a hundred and seventy-two different muscles, but I believe you now. Every one of them is aching."

"They'll ache even more tomorrow," Kuve said cheerfully. "But no matter. They'll soon accustom themselves to the idea that you intend to call on them henceforth."

"I've changed my mind, Kuve. Nature meant me to be the frail, sensitive type."

"Put tomorrow's ordeals out of your mind. At the proper time you'll go through the schedule I've laid out for you. When it's over forget it until it's time to work again."

"I haven't got the will power," Chester said. "I've tried diets and daily dozens before, to say nothing of night classes in which I was going to learn flawless French, or accountancy. It never lasted.''

''The secret of winning disputes with yourself is to refuse to listen. By the time you've perfected your argument you'll be well into your routine. Now let's move along to the dining room. I have a briefing on mnemonics for you, after which I'll start you on pattern theory. Then—''

''When do I sleep?''

''All in good time.''

''Not bad,'' Chester said, finishing off a bowl of clear soup. ''What's next on the menu?''

''Nothing,'' said Kuve. ''But as I was saying, the association of symbol with specific must relate to your personal experience—''

''What do you mean, nothing? I'm a hungry man. I've worked like a draft horse all day!''

''You're overweight, Chester. The soup was carefully compounded to supply the needed nutrients to maintain your energy level.''

''I'll starve.''

''You've been eating from boredom, Chester. When your attention is occupied elsewhere, you forget food. You'll have to master habit.''

''This whole day has consisted of your telling me to mortify the flesh, mind over matter.''

''The mind is the supreme instrument in nature; it must establish its supremacy. I asked you earlier what pain was. What is pleasure?''

''Right now, it's eating!''

''An excellent example: the satisfaction of a natural impulse.''

"It's more than an impulse. It's a necessity! I need more food than a bowl of egg-flower soup without egg flowers!"

"All pleasure impulses, when oversatisfied, become destructive; controlled, the instincts can be very useful. Anger, for example. Here nature has provided a behavioral mechanism to deal with those situations in which aggression seems indicated. It can override other impulses, such as fear. When you are angry, you are stronger, less sensitive to pain, and immune to panic. You desire only to close with your enemy and kill. Before combat males of many species customarily set about working themselves into a rage."

"I'm well on the way."

"You'll learn to control the anger impulse, and evoke it at will without losing control. Now we must move on to the next training situation."

"More?" Chester protested. "I'm exhausted."

"The laziness instinct again," said Kuve. "Come along, Chester."

The sun was setting. Chester and Kuve stood at the base of an eighty-foot tower beside a pool. A steep flight of steps led to a lonely platform at the top.

Kuve handed Chester a small locket. "Climb to the top of the tower. This will enable me to talk to you at a distance. Tomorrow a similar device will be surgically implanted. Now, up you go."

"Let's just go back to that glass floor and pretend some more."

"Simply climb slowly and steadily."

"What's the point in risking my neck up there?"

"Chester, intellectually you are aware that you should co-operate with me. Ignore the distractions of instinct and follow your mind."

"I'll freeze on the ladder. You'll have to send three men up to pry my fingers loose."

"Last week I watched you at the dancing terrace. You sat at a table and ate a large amount of food. You watched the dancers. A girl called to you to join in. You patted your stomach and shook your head."

"What's that got to do with flagpole sitting?"

"The dance they were performing requires great skill and strength and endurance. Had you joined in, would you now enjoy recalling it?"

"Of course, I'd like to be able to—"

"Remembered moments of high achievement satisfy; remembered excesses disgust. Next week will you look back with pleasure on having refused the tower?"

"Not if I fall off and break my neck."

"You have the power to mold your memories—but only before they become memories. This is your opportunity to endow yourself with a recollection worth having."

"Well, just to humor you, I'll start—but I won't guarantee I'll go all the way."

"One step at a time, Chester. Don't look down."

Chester mounted the stairs cautiously, gripping the slender handrail. "This thing wobbles," he called back from ten feet up.

"It will hold. Just keep going."

Chester moved higher. The steps were of wood, eight inches wide and four feet long. The handrail was aluminum, bolted to uprights every fourth step. Chester concentrated his attention on the wood and metal. A buzz sounded from the locket at his throat. "You're going very well. Halfway up now."

The sunset sky flared purple and orange. Chester paused, breathing hard.

"A few more steps, Chester," said the tiny voice in the communicator. He went on. The top of the tower was before him now. Clinging to the rail, he made his way up the last few steps. Far away a twinkle of light showed against the dark forest on the skyline. Red light reflected from a river winding down the valley. The low white building of the Center glowed peach-colored in the fading light. Chester looked down at the pool below.

He dropped flat, eyes shut. "Help!" he croaked.

"Move to the steps, feet first," Kuve said calmly. "Lower your legs, then start down!"

Chester felt the first step under his foot, edged down, one step at a time.

"Halfway down," Kuve's voice said. Chester was moving faster now. At ten feet from the bottom, Kuve halted him.

"Look at the water. Can you jump in from there?"

"Yes, but . . ."

"Go back up a step. Can you jump from there?"

Chester balked three steps higher.

"Jump."

Chester held his nose and sprang into the water. He surfaced, climbed out of the pool.

"Do it again."

After three jumps, Chester went a step higher. Half an hour later, in bright moonlight, he made the jump from twenty feet, whistling down to splash tremendously, then paddling, puffing, to the ladder.

"That's enough for this session," said Kuve. "In a week you'll jump from the top—where you couldn't stand upright today. Now, back inside. While you're getting into some dry garments, I want to talk to you about the nature of reality."

"This is the time of day I usually retire," Chester said, panting. "Couldn't reality wait for tomorrow?"

"You'll have no trouble with insomnia here," Kuve assured him. "By the time you go to bed, you'll be ready to sleep."

In a narrow room with a high window, Chester looked critically at a padded bench three feet wide.

"I'm supposed to sleep on that?"

"There is no mattress like weariness," Kuve said.

Chester kicked off his sandals and lay down with a sigh. "I guess you're right at that, Kuve. I'm going to sleep for a week."

"Four hours," said Kuve. "In addition, you'll have a two-hour nap daily at noon."

There was a buzz from the communicator still on Chester's neck. "Not-is is not is-not," said a soft feminine voice. "Is-not is not not-is. Is is not not-is-not . . ."

"What the devil's this gibberish?"

"The basic axioms of rationality. You'll interpret this material at a subconscious level while you sleep.''

"You mean this is going on all night?"

"All night. But you'll find it doesn't interfere with sleep.''

"What does it mean—is-not is not not-is?"

"This is a simple statement of the nonidentity of symbolic equivalents.''

"Um. You mean 'the map is not the territory.' "

Kuve nodded. "An apparent banality. But by dawn you'll have grasped the implications at a basic level.''

"I won't sleep a wink.''

"If not tonight, then tomorrow," said Kuve, matter-of-factly.

"Not-is-not is not is," the soft voice insisted gently.

"Only three hundred and sixty-four days to go," answered Chester.

7

THE FIRST GRAY of dawn had not yet lighted the sky when Chester tottered into the softly lit gymnasium. Kuve, fresh and immaculate in white, looked up from a small table set up in the middle of the room.

"Good morning, Chester. You slept well?"

"Like a four-day corpse. And I feel equally lively now. I just came to tell you that I'm permanently crippled from yesterday's overexertions. You'd better get a doctor out here. I ought to be in bed, but . . ."

Kuve held up a hand. "Chester, you're expecting me to make much of you and urge you on with inspirational talk. However, I'm afraid we can't spare the time for a pep rally."

"Pep rally? I'm a sick man."

"Still, you're out of bed at the appointed time, dressed for work. And since you're here, you might just take a look at this."

Chester hobbled over to the table. Under a surface of beaded glass, pinpoints of red, green and amber light winked off and on in an unpredictable sequence.

"I want you to analyze the pattern here. When you're ready, put your finger on the button here at the edge which matches the color of the light which you think will blink on next."

Chester studied the light board. A red light blinked, then a green, another red, another, an amber, a green . . . He touched the red light. The board blanked off.

"That means you chose wrongly. Try again with a new pattern." Chester followed the lights. Green, red, amber, red, amber, green, red, green, red . . .

He touched the amber light. The board blanked.

"Never accept the first level of complexity as a solution to a problem, Chester. Look beneath the surface; find the subtler patterns. Try again."

The lights blinked in steady sequence. On Chester's fifth try the entire board lit up. Chester looked pleased.

"Good," said Kuve. "When you have three correct solutions in sequence, we'll move on to patterns of a higher complexity."

"I had to think three lights ahead on the last one, Kuve. The patterns seem to change while I'm watching them."

"Yes, there's a simple developmental progression involved in this set."

"I have more the poetic type mind. I'm no electronic calculator."

"You'll think you are before the year is out. This training, in its advanced phases, by applying pressure of a type never encountered in ordinary experience, will develop cortical areas hitherto unused."

"I don't think I'm going to enjoy that last part," said Chester dubiously. "What does it mean?"

Kuve pointed to the far wall. "Look over there. Keep your eyes rigidly before you." He held up a hand at the edge of Chester's field of vision. "How many fingers am I holding up?"

"I don't know; I can just barely tell there's a hand there."

Kuve waggled a finger. "Did you notice that movement?"

"Certainly."

Kuve moved a second finger, stilling the first, then a third finger, and a fourth.

"You saw the movement each time," he summed up, "which indicates that all four fingers are within your field of view." He extended two fingers. "Now how many fingers am I holding up?"

"I still can't tell."

"You can see the fingers, Chester; you've proven that. And yet you are, quite literally, unable to count these fingers which you see. The message sent to your brain through the portion of the optical mechanism concerned with peripheral vision is channeled to an undeveloped sector of your mind, a part of the great mass of normally unused cells in the cortex. The intelligence of this portion of your intellect is about at a par with that of a faithful dog which recognizes a group of children but is unable to formulate any conception of their number." He lowered his hand. "It is that portion of the brain which we shall train. Now, try this next pattern.''

Chester leaned against the rail at the top of the eighty-foot tower, feeling the sun hot on his shoulders, watching as Kuve adjusted the ropes stretched across the pool below.

''This gives you a four-foot target,'' Kuve's voice said from the rice-grain-sized instrument set in the bone behind Chester's left ear. ''Remember your vascomuscular tension patterns. Wait for the signal.''

A beep sounded in Chester's ear—and he was in the air, wind shrieking past his ears, his chin to his chest, arms extended with hands flat, feet pointed.

He struck, twisted, shot above the surface, swam to the edge, and pulled himself up with a single smooth motion.

''You've come along well these first two weeks,'' Kuve said, motioning Chester to the table where a small steak waited. ''You've explored the parameters of your native abilities; you've established an awareness of the values we're dealing with, and overcome the worst of the metabolic inertia. Your musculature is in good tone, though you still have a long way to go in developing bulk and power. Now you're ready to attack the subtler disciplines of balance, timing, precision, endurance and pace.''

''You make it sound as though I haven't done anything. What about the high dives? That four-foot target isn't very big from eighty feet up.''

''That exercise was designed to develop your self-confidence. Now you'll begin the real substance of your studies. We'll begin with simple games like fencing, riding, rope work, juggling, dancing and sleight-of-hand, and proceed by degrees into the more abstract phases.''

''What are you training me for, a side show?''

Kuve ignored the interruption. ''Your academic studies will be concentrated on dual attention, self-hypnosis, selective concentration, categorical analysis, advanced mnemonics, and eidetics, from which we will proceed to autonomics, cellular psychology, regeneration, and—''

''Let's go back to fencing. At least I know what that is.''

''After you've dined we'll begin. In the meantime, tell me what the word 'now' means.''

'' 'Now' changes,'' said Chester, chewing. ''It moves along with time. Every moment is 'now' for a while, and then it isn't.''

''For a while? How long?''

''Not very long; an instant.''

''Is 'now' a part of the past?''

''Of course not.''

''The future?''

''No, the future hasn't happened yet. The past is already finished. 'Now' falls between them.''

''How would you define a point, Chester?''

''The intersection of two lines,'' Chester said promptly.

''The *position* of intersection, to be more precise,'' said Kuve. '' 'Line' and 'point' are terms referring to positions, not things. If a sheet of paper is cut in two, every molecule of the original sheet is contained in the two halves. If the cut edges are placed together, every particle is still to be found in the two parts; none fall between them.

114

The line we see dividing the halves is only a position, not a material object.''

"Yes, that's obvious."

"Past time may be considered as one of the parts of the paper, future time as the other. Between them is . . . nothing."

"Still, I'm sitting here eating my lunch. Now."

"Your ability to conceptualize falls short of the ability of the universe to proliferate complexities. Human understanding can never be more than an approximation. Avoid dealing in absolutes. And never edit reality for the sake of simplicity. The results are fatal to logical thinking."

Mina appeared on the terrace, wearing a close-fitting pink coverall and carrying foils and face masks. Chester finished his steak, pulled on a black coverall of tough resilient material, took the foil that Mina handed him.

Mina took her position, gripped her slender épée, arm and wrist straight, feet at right angles, left hand on hip. She tapped Chester's blade, then with a sudden flick sent it flying into the pool.

"Oh, I'm sorry, Chester. You weren't ready."

Chester retrieved the foil, assumed a stance in imitation of Mina's. They crossed blades—and Chester oofed as Mina's point prodded his chest. Mina laughed merrily. Chester blushed.

On the third try Mina locked Chester's blade with hers, then, with a twist, plucked it from his hand. ".Chester"—she laughed—"you couldn't be trying." She laid her weapon aside and strolled off. Chester turned to Kuve, face red. Kuve stepped forward, motioned Chester into position.

"We'll have half an hour each morning and

another after lunch," he said. "And," he added softly, "perhaps you'll have a surprise in store for Mina one of these days."

Chester circled Kuve warily, bare feet shuffling on the padded mat. Kuve stepped in, his right hand flashing past Chester's ribs and up to grasp Chester's right wrist, forced back by Kuve's left hand. Chester twisted, caught Kuve's left hand, forced the wrist down. Kuve leaned to relieve the pressure, shifting his hold to Chester's neck, then threw his hip against Chester's side and heaved. In midair Chester brought a leg up, clipped Kuve's jaw with his knee, twisted to land on all fours as Kuve's grip slipped free. Kuve shook his head, looking surprised. "Was that an accident, or . . ."

Chester hit him low, dodged left to avoid a head-lock, clamped an arm over Kuve's head and reached for an ankle—

And was upended and slammed on the mat. He sat up, rubbing his neck. Kuve nodded approvingly. "You're coming along, Chester. If you hadn't been careless with your footwork just now, you might have pinned me."

"Maybe next time," Chester said grimly.

"I seem to note a certain suppressed hostility in your tone," Kuve said, eying Chester with amusement.

"Suppressed, hell. You've worked me like a rented heli for nine months."

"Cheer up, Chester. I have a new compound-reaction test situation for you. It's a very interesting problem group—but I warn you, it can be painful."

"In that respect it fits in nicely with the over-all program."

Chester followed Kuve across the terrace, through an arch, along a corridor, and out into an open court. Kuve pointed to a gate in the wall beyond which a patch of woods pressed close.

"Just go through the gate, Chester, and have a stroll in the forest. You'll find paths; whether you use them is left entirely to your own discretion. This is a tongue of the forest that runs up into the hills. I don't think you'll be in danger of straying too far, for reasons which will become apparent once you're in the forest—but nevertheless I'll caution you to stay close. As soon as you've made what you consider to be a significant observation, return."

Chester glanced toward the shadowed depths of the wood. "My first trip outside the prison grounds. Are you sure I won't run away?"

"Impossible via this route, I'm afraid. If you get into trouble, remember I'll be monitoring your communicator. Be back by dark."

"When in doubt, I'll remember the old school motto: Is-not is not not-is." Chester turned down the path. "Don't wait up for me. I may decide I like it out here."

Chester moved along the path at a steady pace, his eyes roving over his surroundings in a wide-scope comparison pattern.

A movement caught his eye; Chester threw himself backward, feet high. A rope whipped across his calves; then the noose was dangling high in the air. Chester came to his feet carefully, searching for a backup trap, saw none. He studied the tree to which the rope was attached, then moved off the trail to a nearby oak, scaled it quickly, moved out on a long branch, then dropped into the trapped tree. He untied the rope, a tough quarter-inch synthetic, coiled it around his waist, then slid back to the ground.

He moved into the underbrush, froze at a sharp pain in the back of his hand. Carefully he disengaged himself from a loop of fine-gauge barbed wire. Selecting a strand between barbs, he bent it backward and forward rapidly until it parted. He repeated the process with other strands, then went to hands and knees and eased under the barrier.

Half an hour later Chester stood on the brink of a sheer bluff. Fifty feet below, a stream glinted in a shaft of sunlight that fell between great trees. Upstream, a still pool showed black among smooth boulders. Chester noted that its placement was identical with the four-foot target area into which he had been diving daily—an open invitation.

He lay flat and examined the cliff face. The broken rock surface offered an abundance of hand- and foot-holds. Perhaps too many . . .

It was forty feet to the spreading branches of a large elm growing on the opposite side of the stream. Chester uncoiled the rope from his waist, found a five-pound stone fragment with a pinched center, and tied it securely to the end of the supple line. He stood, whirled the stone around his head four times and let it fly. It arched across the branch, dropped and hung swinging. Gently, Chester pulled as the stone swung away, relaxed as it returned, pulled again. The oscillation built up. As the weight started its inward swing, Chester pulled sharply. The stone swung up and over, once, twice, three times around the branch. He tugged; all secure. Quickly he knotted his end of the rope about a length of fallen branch, then man-handled a two-hundred-pound boulder over it. He tested the attachment briefly, then crossed, hand over hand. He left the rope in place, descended to the edge of the quiet pool. Lifting a hundred-pound rock, he tossed it into the center of the black water. Instantly a large net, apparently spring-loaded, snapped into view, dripping water, to close over the stone. Chester smiled, raised his eyes to study the base of the cliff. Snarls of fine barbed wire guarded the lower six feet of the vertical rock face. It would have been an easy climb down, he reflected, but a long way back up.

The communicator behind his ear beeped. "Well, Chester, I see you've sprung the net at the pool. Don't feel too badly; you did very well. I'll be along to release you in a few minutes."

Chester smiled again and turned back into the forest.

Chester studied the sun, briefly reviewed the route he had followed in four hours of detecting and avoiding Kuve's traps. Sunset was just over an hour away, he judged, and he was three miles northwest by north from the Center. He halted, sniffing the air. The odor of wood-smoke was sharp among the milder scents of pine and juniper and sun-warmed rock. He had been climbing steadily for fifty minutes and was ready now to angle to the left to clear the upper end of a ravine. With each step the odor of smoke grew more noticeable. Now a soft gray wisp coiled from the shaded trunks ahead and above. Chester crouched low, moved on quickly. If there was a forest fire ahead, it would be necessary to get past it at once—before he was cut off from his route to the valley. He moved silently through sparse under-brush, saw through a gap in the trees a pale flicker of orange on the heights a hundred yards above. It would be close; he broke into a run.

The trees thinned. The tumbled rocks that marked the head of the gorge showed pale against the dark background of pines. A billow of smoke rolled toward him, carried by a down draft flowing into the canyon. Chester lay flat, drew a dozen deep breaths, then jumped up and scrambled over the broken rock. Ahead, fire twinkled among mas-sive boles, flickered in whipping underbrush, leaped high in the crown of a pine. Hot sparks fell around him. He could hear the roar of wind-driven flames now. A sudden gust blew a wall of smoke toward him. It might be possible, he calculated, to round the knoll at the head of the rampart that edged his route on the right, then descend safely to emerge into the valley a mile north of the Center. There was no hope now of making it before dark. Chester worked his way higher. Another hundred yards—

Twenty feet upslope a heavily built man stepped into view. He was brown-bearded, dressed in patched pants and a loose jacket of faded plaid with three of the four buttons missing. His right hand was at his chin, two fingers hooked around a taut bowstring. The arrow notched in the string carried a four-inch head of polished steel, and it was aimed at Chester's navel.

"I know yew Downlanders move like the snake Demon when the Kez-favver tricked him into the fire pit, but Blew-tewf leaps faster van fought," the bearded man drawled in a barely intelligible dialect. "What yew want here in Free Places? Was life too tame down below?"

Chester frowned, running the sounds of the stranger's barbaric speech through his mind, noting sound substitutions and intonations; the pattern of the dialect was simple.

"If yew don't mind, I'd ravver Blew-tewf pointed over vere somewhere," Chester replied, motioning toward the deep woods, his eyes on the arrowhead. "Yew might just have greasy fingers or somefing of the sort."

"No need to mock the cant," the man said in clear English. "I was ten when I left the Downlands. Now, what do you want here?"

"I was rather hoping to discover a route back to the valley, but I'd settle for merely remaining unskewered and unbroiled. Do you mind if I press on? The fire is blowing this way, you know."

"Don't worry about the fire. I set it myself to run game. It'll burn out against the escarpment above. Now move off to your right and up past me. Blue-Tooth will be watching every move."

"I'm headed in the other direction," Chester said.

"You better do what I told you. Like you said, the fire's gettin' hot." The arrow was still aimed unwaveringly at Chester's stomach. The bow creaked as the bearded man set the arrowhead on the handgrip. "Make up your mind."

"But what in the world do you want with me?"

"Let's say I want news of the Downlands."

"Who are you? What are you doing up here in the hills? If you want news, you could come down to the Center."

"My name's Bandon, and I wouldn't be happy in your blasted Center. Don't turn around, just keep movin' along—and if yew're finkin' of the little trinket tucked away back of your ear, forget it. Yew're out of range."

"You're planning on holding me here for ransom?"

"What treasures could Downlanders offer to equal the life of the Free Places?" Bandon laughed.

"You'll let me go in the morning?"

"Not in the morning or for many a morning vere-after. Forget the tame valleys, Downlander. Yew'll be here until yew die."

8

TWILIGHT WAS FADING from the peaks as Chester and Bandon clambered over the stones of a fallen wall to the level surface of a road that curved between tall poplars toward low buildings silhouetted against the peach-colored sky.

"This is our town, Downlander," Bandon said, breathing hard after the climb. "There's food here, and a fire against the night chill, and strong ale, and the fellowship of free men: all your needs between dusk and dawn."

"Very poetic," Chester said, noting the potholes and weed clumps in the road. "But you left out a few things I've grown accustomed to, like literature, celery, dentists and clean socks. And it looks like some of your houses lack roofs."

"What's a few leaks to a free man?" Bandon snapped.

"Every man to his own little eccentricity," Chester said. "But why do I have to join your club? I'll go quietly."

"Yew came here uninvited," Bandon said flatly He lowered and unstrung his bow. "Don't be foo enough to try to leave. There's sentries posted to guard our approaches."

"I know; I saw them."

"In this light? Our best woodsmen?"

"Just joking," said Chester.

"Maybe you did, at that. You Downlanders are keen-eyed as the Kez-father himself. Tell me, where did you learn the cant?"

"Your dialect? Oh, I . . . ah . . . studied it. A hobby of mine."

"Then it's not true what some say, that you Downlanders can learn our speech in the wink of an eye?"

"A baseless rumor."

"I thought so. Come along now an' we'll see what the brothers make of you." They made their way in the deepening gloom toward the nearest of the buildings. Chester made out the details of chipped carving around doorways, fallen trellises, collapsed porticos. A broken statue lay in the road.

"This must have been a pretty nice town, once," Chester said. "What happened to it?"

Bandon snorted. "We threw off all those slave notions about drudging away to put on a show for the neighbors. We're free here. No one to tell us what to do. Folks that didn't like the idea moved out. Good riddance. We don't need 'em."

"Swell," Chester agreed. "But what happens when it gets cold?"

"Plenty wood around here. We build fires."

Chester eyed the blackened foundation of a

burned-out house. "I see . . ."

"That was an accident," Bandon growled. "Plenty more houses where that came from." He stopped. "Hold it right here." He threw back his head and whistled shrilly. From doorways and dark hedges and the shadows of ragged trees, men appeared.

Chester estimated the crowd of unshaven, hide-clad hill-dwellers who surrounded him at fifty individuals, all male—none of them, he reflected, of the kind who would arouse a desire for further acquaintance.

"Vis Downlan'er's a guest," Bandon was saying to the assembled brethren. "We'll treat him as one of us—unless he tries tew go somewhere. Now, I'm takin' him in the palace wiv me—jus' until he can get a place of his own fix' up. I warn yew now: if he comes tew harm, I'll hol' the lot of yew personally responsible."

A tall, incredibly broad man in striped coveralls black with dirt swaggered forward. "We heard a lot about how tough vese Downlanders are," he growled. "Vis one don't look so tough."

"Maybe he's smart—vat's better yet," Bandon snapped. "Leave him alone, Grizz. Vat's an order."

Grizz looked around at his fellows. "Funny none of us is good enough tew get tew sleep in the palace. But vis spy here walks in an' right away he's treated like the Kez-favver hisself when he went tew fetch the king hat back from the sea bottom."

"Never mind vat. Now yew boys get a fire goin' in the Hall and roast up some venison and break open a few kegs of ale. We're goin' tew have a real celebration here tew show the new man what kind of jolly free life we lead.''

A few shouts rang out, a faint yippee sounded from the rear. Grizz stared at Bandon. "We got no venison. Plenty canned beans and stale crackers. Only ale we got is a couple cases of near-beer Lonny stole last week.''

"Dew the best yew can,'' Bandon snapped. "Look lively about it. I want tew see yew lookin' cheerful around here.'' He turned to Chester and motioned toward an imposing facade featuring chipped columns and broken glass. "Come along tew the palace; yew'll have a chance tew get cleaned up before the feast.''

"Jus' a minute,'' Grizz said. He stepped up to Chester, brought an iron bar into view.

"I warned you, Grizz,'' Bandon started.

"I won' hurt him—yet.'' Grizz growled. He gripped the bar at either end, hunched his shoulders and strained. The metal gave, bent to a crude U. He let out his breath, shoved the bar at Chester.

"Straighten it, Swamp-walker.''

"Not in the mood,'' Chester said mildly.

Grizz barked a laugh, dropped the bar with a clatter, stepped to the roadside and came back with a massive chunk of carved stone. "Here, catch.'' He heaved the boulder toward Chester, who moved his foot barely in time as the rock crashed down.

Bandon strung his bow with a quick motion. "Vat's enough, Grizz,'' he snapped. "Come along, Downlan'er.''

126

"I'll be seein' yew, Swamp-walker," Grizz called after them.

Chester followed Bandon across a littered stone terrace, past gaunt paint-peeling doors into an echoing interior that smelled of stale hides and forgotten food scraps. A broken-down sofa leaned in one corner beside a table with a bandaged leg. A heap of bedding sprawled by a wide fireplace stacked with splintered chair rungs. A staircase with a broken banister curved up past a glassless window to a gallery.

"The place looks a little run-down," Chester commented. "Who used to live here?"

"Dunno." Bandon took a lighter from his pocket, snapped it until it caught. " 'Bout out of fluid," he said. "Used to be some boss types lived here, but when we wouldn't take orders, they just moved out—had to get down in the flatlands to get fitted for chains, I guess."

"What kind of orders?"

"Oh, you know. Always wantin' to set up a committee to patch roofs or clean gutters or string wire. Dirty work."

"I think perhaps they had some reason on their side," Chester said, looking around at peeling wallpaper and decayed curtains.

"Heck, they should've done all that themselves. But no, they ran off and left it. We locked up a few of 'em and tried to make 'em work, but they got loose somehow."

"The boss caste is sneaky, all right," Chester said. "Always fooling us fun-loving folks by knowing something we don't."

"Durn right," Bandon agreed.

"Why don't you gather firewood in the forest instead of burning the furniture?" Chester asked. "There's no place to sit."

"Sure there is. Just look under that pile of hides there. We tried burning sticks, but they don't burn so good. This stuff's nice and dry. Now, soon's we have a cheery blaze goin', we'll have a talk about conditions down below. Still the same old slave life, I suppose: everybody minding everybody's else's business."

"Uh-huh," Chester said, glancing over the assorted debris scattered on the floor. "They're still burdened down with swimming pools and laundries and picnics and concerts and all manner of frivolity. By the way, where do the canned beans and crackers come from?"

"Plenty of stores here," Bandon said, dipping water from a barrel and pulling off his shirt. "Lots of stuff in 'em. The boys could turn up some good eats if they half tried." He splashed water on his face and chest, snorted, dabbed at himself with the shirt, then pulled it back on.

"O.K., it's all yours," he said. Chester eyed the brown water dubiously. "What happens when the stores are looted clean?"

"We've got plans," Bandon said darkly. "We won't starve." He shoved rubbish from a slack-twisted chair and seated himself. "I happen to have a couple of bottles of Tricennium brew tucked away," he said. "Soon's you're washed up, we'll have 'em. Wouldn't do to let on to the boys; not enough to go around."

"That's the spirit," Chester said. "I think I'll

defer bathing until later."

"Huh! I thought you Downlanders were great ones for washin' off. Heck, I wash off myself all the time, like you just saw me do."

"You have a great instinct for personal daintiness," Chester said tactfully. "An admirable quality. Tell me, why all the emphasis on rugged individuality? Did someone take away your pet goat when you were a lad?"

"Worse'n that," Bandon said. "They used to try to make my pa do their dirty work for 'em. He didn't take kindly to it. He organized the Resistance. Now look." Bandon waved a hand in a proud gesture. "It's all mine—mine and the boys'."

"I can see you're not one to keep off a lawn just because somebody else planted it and keeps it mowed," Chester said admiringly. "Strictly self-sufficient. You just live in these old houses that happened to grow here and you eat wholesome, natural canned beans, the way the Lord intended, and you loot your clothes right out of Mother Nature's own abandoned dry-goods stores. To heck with maintenance. When this town wears out, there's always plenty of others."

"You can lay off the smart talk," Bandon said. "We've got as much right as anybody to live soft."

"Sure—just because some smart-aleck invented something and some exploiter built a factory to make it and some wisenheimer did the engineering, that's no reason you shouldn't wake up from your nap long enough to get your share. And now let's have that ale you were talking about. If I'm going to spend the rest of my life here, I'll have to start getting used to drinking it warm.''

''Yew'll like it fine, after you get used to it,'' Bandon said. He went to a doorless refrigerator, lifted the lid and rummaged, came up with two brown bottles. Chester wandered around the room, noting the remains of a grandfather's clock, a gutted washing machine filled with firewood, a coil of clothesline, some picture wire, a scatter of rusted nails, bent coat-hangers, burst cardboard boxes, wadded clothing.

''What have you got against the conveniences of life, Bandon?'' he asked, accepting a bottle. ''What would be wrong with, say, cleaning this room up so it smelled as good as the woods outside of town? Is there anything particularly independent about keeping your discarded junk in the living room?''

''We don't care anything about setting up fancy places to live in. We prefer a kind of nice informal look.''

''You're echoing a long line of philosophers who concluded that the secret of the universe consisted of sitting around in your own dirt—all the way from early Christians to twentieth-century beatniks. I can be just as self-righteous as the next fellow, while I'm sitting in an air-conditioned restaurant ordering *haute cuisine* with one hand and lighting up an expensive dope stick with the other, with a well-stacked young lady occupying the rest of my attention. The point is, why not be virtuous in comfort?''

''Look here, don't go trying to spread discontent around among my men.''

"Your men? I thought you were all free as bed-bugs in the railroad men's Y."

"We are. But any outfit needs a little organization. Don't you get the boys upset—otherwise I might just give Grizz the go-ahead."

"I have a disturbing conviction that Grizz may not wait for the go-ahead. He seems to resent me."

"Don't worry; I'll keep an eye on him." Bandon finished off his bottle. "Let's join the boys. I guess things ought to be rollin' pretty good by now. Just stay close—and yell if you need help."

Chester followed Bandon down the wide, rubble-littered front steps into the street and across into a large, garishly lighted ex-restaurant, to survey a scene of half-hearted festivity. A blaze in the fireplace dispelled the evening chill. Around it, the brothers stood, hands in pockets, muttering. At sight of Bandon and Chester, the massive figure of Grizz detached itself from the bar.

"Well, the new man's been makin' hisself comfortable," he said loudly. "Say, I hear yew Downlanders are fast. I wonder if . . ."

Grizz made a sudden movement. Chester put up a hand and the bone handle of a hunting knife slapped his palm, fell to the ground.

"Here, Grizz, yew had no call tew frow a knife at our guest!"

"Never mind, Bandon," Chester said easily. "He was just kidding."

"Lucky yew happen' tew stick out yewr han' jus' when yew did," Bandon said. "It was comin' butt first, but it would have hurt. Grizz, leave him alone." Bandon slapped Chester on the back.

"I've got tew circulate around a little, talk tew a few of the boys. Yew get acquainted tew." He moved off.

There was a step behind Chester. He eased aside and half turned. Grizz thrust heavily through the spot he had just vacated. The nearby men moved back, fanning out. Chester stood looking up at Grizz. The mountaineer was at least seven feet tall.

"We don't take much tew spies," Grizz growled.

"I can see why," said Chester. "If the other half knew what you boys had all to yourselves up here, they'd leave home tomorrow."

"Vere's a way tew handle swamp-walkers," Grizz stated, rubbing his right fist in his left palm.

"Vat's right, Grizz," a voice called.

"Show him, Grizz," another suggested.

"Now, Bandon says treat vis swamp-walker like one of the boys." Grizz looked around. Heads nodded reluctant agreement.

"But what if maybe vis guy jumps me? I fight back, right?"

"Shewre yew dew!"

"Yew ain' a man tew back down, Grizz!"

"I seen him dew it!"

There was a sound behind Chester. He stepped casually to one side; a man stumbled past the spot on which Chester had been standing, blundered into Grizz. With a snarl, Grizz pushed aside the man who had jostled him, stepped to Chester, and threw a tremendous punch—as Chester looked the other way, leaned toward the fire. The blow brushed his neck. Chester seemed not to notice.

He rubbed his hands together. "Nice blaze," he commented brightly. He took a step away from Grizz, still not looking at him, moved a chair aside with a deft motion.

Grizz stumbled over the chair leg, fell full length. Chester looked startled, bent to help Grizz up. "Excuse me, Grizz old boy." He made ineffectual brushing motions at Grizz, who came to his feet, hamlike fists doubled, as Chester stooped, came up with Grizz's knife.

Grizz froze, eyes on the blade.

"Guess you'll be needing this," Chester said, holding it out.

Grizz hesitated, then snarled and turned away.

"Nobody could be that clumsy—and that lucky," a voice said softly. Chester turned. Bandon stood eying him uncertainly. "But on the other han', nobody could be that fast and that smooth—if they were doin' it on purpose."

"A grand bunch of fellows," said Chester. "I'm feeling right at home."

"You're a strange one," Bandon said. "I've got a feeling maybe it's Grizz who better be careful."

"I hope he never gets a good grip on me," Chester said. "I'm afraid I'd bend into a U before Grizz realized the danger he was in. I think I'll take a stroll outside."

Bandon grunted and turned away. Chester went out into the street, his shadow pushing before him. A man stepped from shelter of an ornamental fountain, bow in hand. Chester angled off to the right; a second man appeared, weapon ready.

"Just checking, fellows," Chester said. He sauntered back, strolled fifty yards toward the dark woods before sentries appeared silently. He stopped, admired the view while the guards waited, then retraced his steps to the Hall.

"Time to eat," Bandon called. "Grizz was just talkin' mean," he confided when Chester came up. "We've got plenty of good stuff here. Try these sardines."

Chester eyed the soggy fish. "I'm afraid they're not a favorite of mine. I'll wait for the game course."

"Salami on crackers?" Bandon suggested. "We cut off the bad part."

"Any fruit—or berries?" Chester suggested. "Or nuts?"

"That's stuff for squirrels and rabbits," Bandon said shortly. "Hey, after the feast, we're all goin' to have a little shindig. You'll enjoy it."

"Ah, the true joys of the free life at last. What do you do, sing rousing songs, dance horn pipes, exchange buffets, all that sort of thing?"

"Heck, no. We view television. There's some dandy historicals about the old times, when men were men."

"I see. It's a sort of indoctrination program."

"Look here, you might as well quit smartin' off. I tell you, this is the life. After a few years, you'll start to see what I mean."

"It's not the years, it's the next few hours that bother me. I dislike Tri-D intensely. Suppose I go back and tidy up your quarters for you while you enjoy the free life."

"Suit yourself. You can't get away. I'll see that Grizz stays at the show so you can relax."

"Thanks. I'll try to arrange things at your place

to give a more fitting reception to any unexpected callers who might drop in.''

9

IT WAS THREE hours since the last sounds of revelry had died. In the palace, Chester sat awake, watching the red glow of the fireplace, and listening. In the corner Bandon snored softly on his pallet. Far away, a night bird called. Something creaked faintly near the door.

Chester crossed the room to Bandon, called his name softly. He grumbled, opened his eyes. "Hah?"

Chester put his face close to Bandon's. "Quiet," he breathed. "Grizz is at the door."

Bandon started up. Chester held him by a hand on his arm. "Let him in. It's better to take him here . . . alone."

"He wouldn't dare push his way into the palace," Bandon whispered.

"Stay where you are." Chester moved silently to the door, stood beside it in the dark. There was a rasping sound, very faint. Then the door moved an inch, paused for a full minute, moved again. From his place behind the heavy door post, Chester saw Grizz's small eyes and bushy beard. Then the door moved wider; Grizz stepped inside, closed the door soundlessly. As he turned back toward the bed where Bandon lay, Chester rammed the stiff fingers of his left hand into Grizz's stomach, then, as Grizz jackknifed forward, struck him back-handed under the ear with the side of his fist. Grizz fell with a heavy slam.

Bandon was on his feet now. "Don't give the alarm, Bandon," Chester whispered. "There's nobody to hear it but his henchmen."

Bandon said hoarsely, "What did he want here? How do you know—"

"Shhh. Grizz was after both of us, Bandon. If he knifed me, he'd have to finish you, too—or face Blue-Tooth later."

"You're ravin'. My people are loyal—includin' Grizz."

"Grizz was listening this evening when we were talking. He was afraid you'd be influenced. That gave him all the excuse he needed. So . . . here he is."

"You come here to make trouble," Bandon grated. "Like Grizz said."

Chester pointed to a heap of uncured hides behind the crude table. "Conceal yourself over there and listen."

Bandon reached up suddenly, took his bow from its peg on the wall, nocked the steel-tipped arrow. "I'll hide," he said. "An' this will be pointed straight at you—so don't try any tricks."

"Be careful with that. I'd hate to be skewered by accident."

Grizz was beginning to stir. Bandon stepped from sight in the shadows.

Grizz sat up, shook his head, got clumsily to his feet. He stood swaying, looked around the silent cabin and saw Chester, almost at his feet, curled up in the bed of rags, snoring lightly.

Grizz half crouched, pig eyes darting around the room. He took a knife from his belt, dug a moc-casined toe into Chester's side. Chester rolled on his back, opened his eyes and sat up.

"Where's Bandon?" Grizz growled, the long blade tilted toward Chester's throat.

"Oh, hi there," said Chester. "Say, I hope you're O.K. now after your fall."

"I said where's Bandon?"

Chester looked around. "Isn't he here?"

"He slugged me and got away. Now, talk, Swamp-walker. What are yew tew love birds plannin'?"

Chester chuckled. "He's the chief here; I'm just a captive Downlander, remember?"

"Yew're a liar on bofe counts. Yew fink I'm dumb enough not tew see frew vis setup? The tew of yew are in somefing tewgevver. Where's he gone?"

"If I help you, will you let me go?"

"Shewre."

"You promise? I'll have safe-conduct back to the valley if I tell you where Bandon is so you can kill him?"

"Yeah, I promise. Safe-conduct. Yew bet."

"How do I know you'll keep your promise?"

"Are yew sayin' I'm a liar?" Grizz leaned closer with the knife.

"Careful. I haven't told you yet."

"Yew got my word on it: yew go free. Where is he?"

"Well . . ." Chester came to his knees. "He's on his way back to my Tricennium. He discovered you were taking over here, so he—"

"Fanks, sucker!" Grizz lunged with the knife. Chester threw himself back, yanking at a tripwire; a bucket of sand dropped from a rafter and took Grizz in mid-leap. He slammed the floor face first. Chester came to his feet holding the knife Grizz had dropped. Grizz moved groggily, shaking his head.

"Looks like you're a promise-breaker after all, Grizz," Chester said, moving in with the long blade ready.

Grizz scrabbled backward, one hand up to ward off a thrust. "Don't dew it, don't dew it!" he squalled.

"Keep your voice down. If anyone barges in, you'll be the first to go." Chester stood over Grizz. "Now, what about that promise you made? You were going to give me safe-conduct."

"Shewre. I'll see yew get away clean. Just leave it to me."

"I could kill you, Grizz. But that wouldn't get me out of here." Chester looked worried. "Suppose I let you go. Will you give me an escort down to the valley?"

"Shewre I will, yew bet I will, fella. I just got excited when yew said Bandon was on his way down."

"Well, I guess I'll give you another chance." Chester put the knife in his belt. "But remember, you've given me your word."

"Vat's right, my word on it, fella."

"I've got to get a couple of things . . ." Chester turned away. In a lithe movement Grizz rolled to hands and knees, snatched up a rusted hatchet lying conveniently by, sprang at Chester's back.

And slammed face first into the hard-packed earth floor as his toe hooked the wire Chester had stretched across the room at ankle height.

Chester turned, looked down sadly at Grizz. "You did it again, Grizz. Dear, oh dear. I'm afraid I have no choice but to cut your throat, since you're not to be trusted."

"Look," whined Grizz, scraping dirt from his face. "I figured you wrong, see? I made a mistake."

"You certainly did," Chester said coldly. He moved closer, reached out and set the point of the blade under Grizz's chin. "One sudden move, and in it goes. How would it feel, Grizz? They say a really keen edge feels cold as it slices through. There wouldn't be too much pain, but breathing would get rather difficult, and, as the blood drained out of you, you'd get weak. In a few seconds you'd be unable even to stand. You'd just lie there and feel the life dwindle in you."

"Don't hurt me," Grizz gasped. "I'll dew anything."

"Who sent you here?" Chester snapped.

"Joj did. He's the one. He planned it all."

"Tell me about it."

"Vere's over a fousand of us. We've got steel crossbows, even chemical bombs." Grizz outlined plans for a raid on the nearest Tricennium. "It's planned for free days from now," he finished. "Vey haven't got a chance against us. But yew . . . yew let me up now, no hard feelings, and I'll see yew get yewr share. What ever yew want—slaves, women . . ."

"No point in my going back now," said Chester thoughtfully. "I don't want to be there when the massacre takes place." He straightened, the knife still ready. "My best bet is to go along with you. I'm pretty good with a knife, Grizz. If I join you, do my share of the killing, will you pay off as you suggested?"

"Absolewtly. Yew can trust me now. I've learned my lesson." Grizz eyed the knife as Chester tossed it aside and put out his hand.

"We'll shake on that, Grizz."

Grizz came to his feet, reaching for Chester's hand, and with a tremendous surge spun him around, threw a whistling left at the back of Chester's neck that somehow failed to connect solidly, followed up with a right cross that Chester somehow managed to avoid. Chester went down and Grizz was on him, his two hundred and forty pounds of muscle and bone crushing Chester flat, while two thumbs like bolt-cutters probed Chester's Adam's apple.

"Now, Swamp-walker," Grizz breathed, "what was vat about lettin' blood out of me? Cut my froat, would yew? Feels cool, hey? How dew yew reckon it's gonna be when I put the fumbs in hard?"

"You gave me your word," Chester wheezed.

"I kept my part of the bargain." He groped, found the loop of clothesline he had prepared and flipped it into position.

"I don't bargain wif Downlander spies. I tear 'em intew strips, barehanded."

"I let you go when I could have killed you," Chester got out. "Now let me up and give me my escort." With a quick flip, he dropped the loop over Grizz's head.

Grizz hardly noticed in his enthusiasm. "Yew fink I'm stupid? I've got plans for yew, Swamp-runner," he said, releasing his grip with one hand to tug at the loose noose. "Ever felt a bone break—slow?"

"You mean you're breaking your promise?"

"Yew catch on quick."

Chester looked up at Grizz's puffed face, the wide mouth among the wiry whiskers, the small eyes. He tugged on the line. An expression of surprise crept over Grizz's face. His back straightened, his head rising. He dug in his thumbs frantically, but Chester twisted away. Then Grizz was struggling to get his legs under him, his hands raking at the wire that was hoisting him up neck first.

Chester slid back, keeping pressure on the wire which ran over a rafter to the loop on Grizz's throat. Grizz scrambled to get his feet under him. "You're a very slow pupil, Grizz." Chester jerked the wire. Grizz's head bobbed. Chester hauled on the wire, then twisted it around a stout peg set in a massive post. Grizz stood on tiptoes, breathing rapidly, his eyes bulging, his head tilted sideways by the taut wire, his fingers groping fruitlessly at the noose buried in the fleshy neck.

Chester stood before him, hands on hips. "I guess I'll just hang you, Grizz," he said. "Less messy than cutting your throat."

"Please," Grizz whispered past the constricting wire. "Give me another chance."

"Have you learned your lesson?"

"Yeah, cut me down."

"Remember, it's no use trying to double-cross me. Now just give me an escort like a good fellow . . ." Chester released the wire. Grizz clawed the noose free, threw it aside, stood rubbing his throat and staring at Chester. Chester stood six feet from him, hands empty, looking at him casually. "Well, you're free now, Grizz. What about your promise?"

Grizz felt carefully about his head and neck, ran his hands over his arms, leaned to check his ankles, his eyes fixed on Chester.

"Oh, it's quite all right now, Grizz. There are no more wires attached to you."

Grizz glanced down, pushed out a foot to check for trap wires. He licked his lips.

"Don't do anything foolish, Grizz. I've warned you. I'm in control of you, not the other way around. The sooner you accept that . . ."

Grizz leaped, caught a tight-stretched wire square in the mouth and did a complete back flip.

"Get up!" Chester snapped. Grizz got to his feet, hands hanging at his sides, staring at Chester.

"Yours is the typical bully attitude," said Chester. "Anyone you consider to be stronger than you is your master; anyone who seems to be at your mercy becomes your victim. You've had a little trouble classifying me: I seemed to be a victim but repeatedly demonstrated that it was you who was being victimized. Are you ready now to accept reality?''

Grizz stood dumbly. Chester reached out, gripped the other's nose and twisted hard. Grizz gulped. Chester prodded him in the stomach, thumped his chest, kicked him lightly in the shin. ''Well, care to try again?'' Grizz swallowed hard, mouth opening and closing.

''I think perhaps you're properly oriented now, Grizz. You may go. Tell everyone that the attack has been postponed and that they're to stay clear of the palace. Don't tell anyone what happened here. Understand?''

Grizz nodded.

''And, Grizz, don't try to cheat on me.''

There was a sound. Bandon stepped into view, the arrow aimed at Grizz's chest. ''You intend to let this traitor walk out of here and warn 'em?''

''Hold on, Bandon. He won't give any trouble.''

''Not if I can help it.'' Bandon made a sudden move and Chester whirled, snapped a hand out—

And stood gripping the shaft of the arrow, caught in mid-flight.

''You—you grabbed my Blue-Tooth's dart out of the air!'' Bandon stared at Chester incredulously. ''It's not possible!''

''Accept reality,'' Chester said. ''It's simply a matter of trained reflexes and self-hypnotic alert conditioning.''

''But then—when I brought you in—you could have . . .''

''That's right—but I wanted to see what was

going on up here. Now we both know. We'd better move out now—fast. Grizz will snap out of his daze in a few minutes, and you'll discover how loyal your boys are."

"But . . . why should they want to turn on me? All I've done's been for their own good."

"Maybe—but the one thing your little group has in common is a yearning for more free goodies and less work. All anybody has to do to enlist their enthusiasm is promise them some easy loot."

"Hold on; I don't know what Grizz has said to them, but I can—"

"Promise them more," Chester finished. "But can you deliver? This is a dead end, Bandon. Come on with me."

"I'm still boss here." Bandon said. "Come on; you'll see." He started for the door.

"Do me a small favor," Chester said, tucking the rusted hatchet into his waistband. "Sneak out the back way and look the situation over before you do anything foolish. I'm leaving now. I have a trail of unfinished business to see to. I hope you won't try to interfere."

Bandon hesitated. "I guess I owe you something," he said. "Grizz was out to get me, sure. But you're makin' a mistake. The free life is the only way."

Chester coiled the clothesline and looped it in his belt. "If you were smart, you'd head for the nearest Center and get used to clean clothes and a good bed again. You don't belong here with these wood lice. Leave this routine to Grizz and the other wild life."

"I'm safe enough. Come on with me. I'll give

you a safe-conduct through the lines."

"Sorry, Bandon; I don't think you could guarantee that. I'm taking the back way."

"There's nothin' back there but the cliff face. You can't get through my sentry lines. There's too many men out there. You can't catch five arrows at once—and some of the boys have powder guns."

"I know—so that just leaves me one way out."

"Up the escarpment? You can't climb that—it's straight up."

"I don't have a lot of choice. Sorry you're not going with me. But if you change your mind, there's a cleft just behind the third house from the corner. I'll start from there."

"Got it all figured out, eh? You Downlanders beat me. Well, suit yourself."

"Thanks. And keep your head down until you see which way the wind is blowing."

10

IN THE BLACKNESS of Bandon's back yard, Chester paused, listening. A soft wind moved in the tall pines. Small frogs called; a bird shrilled again and again. Chester moved across the weed-choked garden, worked his way through a wild-grown hedge and over a fallen fence, started up a gravelly slope. Starlight gave a faint illumination. Behind him there was a sudden voice in the street, an angry retort. Chester recognized Bandon's voice. He reached the base of the cleft, found handholds, started up. Yells sounded from below now and Grizz's bull roar. Chester pulled himself up to a ledge and turned, waiting. The voices went on; then the thump of running feet sounded, coming nearer.

"Over here," Chester called softly. He picked up a fist-sized rock, hefted it. Hoarse breathing sounded below, the scrabble of feet on gravel.

"Bandon?" Chester said softly.

"It's me," a choked voice came back. "Why,

those lousy, miserable, ungrateful skunks!"

"Uh-huh," Chester said. "Hurry up." He tossed the rock aside, unlimbered the coil of tough clothesline. Other feet sounded now. A torch flared behind Bandon's house.

Grizz's voice bellowed commands: "Beat vat brush, boys. Ve turncoat can't be far off!"

There was a sound of sliding, followed by a thump. Below, Bandon cursed in a strained whisper. "How in the name of the Kez-father do you get up there?"

"Hey, I heard somefing over vere," a voice called. A second torch flared.

Chester tied a loop in the end of the clothesline, lowered it down the cleft. "Grab this," he whispered. "And keep it quiet."

Bandon muttered softly to himself; Chester felt the rope move as Bandon fumbled with it. "Hurry up!" Chester called.

"Haul away," Bandon said softly. Chester braced his feet and pulled. Bandon's feet scraped, sent small stones rattling down the rock face.

"Over vere!" two voices yelled at once. Pounding feet approached. There was a yelp and one torch went out.

"Somebody found my coon trap," Bandon grunted. With a final heave, Chester hauled him up high enough to grip the edge of the ledge. A moment later, they stood side by side.

"I'm going on up," Chester said. "Don't make a sound. As soon as I reach secure footing again, I'll lower the line."

"Don't waste any time," Bandon said, "Grizz may not be able to climb up here, but he's a pretty good hand with a long bow. A pure shame I didn't have time to gather up my Blue-Tooth.''

''All you'd do is get us spotted quicker. Stand fast now.'' Chester reached up, found a grip, pulled himself up. The going was easy enough; the fingerholds were all of a quarter of an inch deep, and the climb was not even quite vertical; there was a slope of at least three degrees. As for the height, it was negligible: a mere sixty feet or so now. A few months ago, it would have been a different story, Chester thought suddenly, smiling. In the old days, he would have clung to the cliff, bleating for help.

Abruptly, the precariousness of his position dawned on Chester. What was he, Chester W. Chester IV, doing here, climbing up the face of a vertical precipice in the dark, with a crew of ferocious back-to-nature cultists at his heels? Suddenly, the meager handholds seemed grossly inadequate. Chester froze, digging with his toes for a secure footing. The light breeze seemed to batter at him like a gale. His shoulder blades drew together in anticipation of Grizz's long-bow bolt.

''Hey,'' Bandon's voice whispered anxiously from below. ''Don't forget me.''

Chester drew a deep breath and let it out slowly, feeling his fear-tensed muscles loosen. He was glad Kuve hadn't been around to see how easily he'd forgotten his training in a moment of panic. He went up another ten feet, found a foot-wide ledge and lowered the rope. There were three torches below now, near the foot of the cliff.

''Here's some footprints,'' someone called.

''Hey, look up vere,'' another voice shouted.

"Did you see somefing move?"

"It's him!"

"Who's got a bow handy?"

"Bandon," Chester called softly. "Gather up a handful of rocks, then tie the rope around your waist. You pepper 'em while I pull you up. Maybe it will be enough to spoil their aim—or at least make them nervous."

"Sure."

Chester heard the rasp of stone, then a grunt as Bandon pegged one. There was a loud yell from below.

"Got the skunk!" Bandon whispered loudly. A moment later a second cry rang out.

"What's goin' on?" someone wanted to know.

"Rocks fallin'."

"Ohhh, my head!"

"Bandon, hurry up! Get that rope tied!" Chester felt the rope vibrate.

"All right," Bandon called. Chester heaved at the rope. It was hard work this time, with Bandon too fully occupied to assist by clawing his way up as Chester pulled. The rope cut into Chester's hands. An arrow clanged against the stone ten feet to one side, striking red sparks. Chester grunted and hauled. More arrows struck, one no more than a yard away. One of the torches below went out as its bearer yelled.

"Don't throw at the torches," Chester gasped. "All they do is blind them."

"Oh, sorry," Bandon said cheerfully. "The varmints are thick as fleas in a bearhide down there. Can't hardly miss."

He crawled up beside Chester. "Whoosh! That

rope cuts! And we've still got a ways to go.'' An arrow ricocheted off the rock wall a yard from Chester's head.

''Let's get out of here. They'll bracket in on us before long. If you're hit, try not to yell.''

''I'll keep 'em busy,'' Bandon said. He stooped, came up with head-sized stone, and dropped it down into the darkness. It hit once with a crash; a moment later three hoarse yells sounded almost together.

''Ha!'' Bandon exulted. ''That's showin' 'em.''

Three painful climbs and half an hour later Chester and Bandon lay stretched full-length on a wide ledge. The noise below had dwindled to an occasional half-hearted curse and a few groans. The arrows had stopped coming.

''Looks like we got away clean,'' Bandon said. ''The skunks sure gave up easy.''

''We'll rest a few minutes,'' Chester said. ''Then we'll go on to the top and head back toward the Center—''

''Oh-oh,'' Bandon said.

''What's the matter?''

''Reckon I forgot somethin'.''

''Well, I don't think we'd better go back for it, under the circumstances.''

''It's not that. But I forgot to tell you. This cliff we've gone and climbed up on: no wonder the boys aren't too worried about gettin' after us.''

''Well?''

''There's no way down. If you'd seen it in daylight you'd know what I mean. It's a mesa, and the side we're climbing is the easy one.''

Hot morning sun beat down on Chester's short-cropped head as he walked along the cliff edge to the boulder against which Bandon sat waiting.

"It's like I told you," Bandon said. "We're stuck."

"Why didn't you mention the topographical peculiarities of the place to me last night, when I first announced I was heading this way?" Chester asked.

"I figured it wouldn't matter, 'cause I didn't figure you'd be able to get up here anyhow. I figured you'd be back in a few minutes, beggin' my pardon and askin' for that safe-conduct. I guess I made kind of a fool of myself."

"I won't be so uncivil as to argue that point." Chester peered over the precipice. It dropped vertically for fifty feet, then shelved back. The base was visible a hundred yards below, plunging sheer into a green blanket of treetops.

"Grizz'll have the boys spotted all the way around, the trip wires rigged," Bandon said. "Even if we had a way to get down, they'd be on top of us like flies on a beer keg before we got our shirt tails tucked in."

Chester scaled a rock out over the forest, watched it curve and drop down, down . . .

"Poor Genie," he said. "And Case."

"I don't know who you're grievin' over," Bandon said, "but you can add your own name to the list. If we don't starve up here, it'll be because we climbed down and broke our necks—or got plugged full of arrows. One thing we don't have to do is get heat stroke. Let's get over under the trees."

They walked across the stony ground toward the rising mound of wooded land that occupied the center of the ten-acre island of the mesa top.

"We'd better look around and see if there's anything edible growing up here," Chester said.

"And water," Bandon added. "I'm already gettin' thirsty."

"Maybe we can find some game. Why don't you set to work and make yourself a new bow? I'll start on a shelter, in case it rains—and we'll have to rig some sort of catch-basin, if we don't find a spring."

"What's the use? It'll just stretch out our dyin'. Maybe we ought to just take a flyin' jump. Maybe we'd land on a couple of Grizz's skunks."

"Here, none of that," Chester said sharply. "We may find that we can live quite comfortably here—in spite of the lack of canned beans and television. This is your opportunity to try the free life you're so fond of."

"Sure, but . . ." Bandon muttered.

"You start off in that direction." Chester pointed toward a stand of slender, bluish-needled conifers. "I'll check over there. We'll meet back here at the edge of the woods in an hour."

Chester laid aside the rusted hatchet with which he had been pounding in a stake.

"Any luck?" he called as Bandon tramped from the underbrush.

"I guess so," Bandon said dispiritedly. "There's a good stand of ash back there I can make some kind of bow out of. And I found some kind of an old tent—"

Chester came to his feet. "You mean the place is inhabited?"

Bandon shook his head. "Not any more. Come on. I need help to get it out. We can use the material to build that catch-basin, and I guess there's enough over to put a roof on that hut of yours." He nodded toward Chester's embryonic framework of sticks bound together with lengths of clothesline wire.

Chester followed Bandon back into the woods, pushing through tangled underbrush, squeezing between interlaced saplings. The taller trees became thicker and the ground more open as they progressed. Ahead, draped in the branches of a dead pine, Chester saw a billow of grayish-white, a snarl of lines trailing down almost to the ground.

"There it is," Bandon said. "Don't know what it's doin' in a treetop. But there's plenty of stuff there to make a hut and whatever else we need. And some good rope, too. Not that it's goin' to do us any good," he added.

"It's a parachute," Chester said in wonder. "I was under the impression that there were no aeronautics here, other than helis, and you don't need parachutes with those. They let themselves down gently if the power fails."

"What other kind is there?" Bandon inquired.

Chester explained to Bandon the function of a conventional flying machine.

"I never heard of any such thing," Bandon said, shaking his head. "But it seems like I remember some kind of big gas bag some fellows put on some kind of show with, once when I was a kid back in the Tricennium. They went sailin' right up into the sky. Damnedest thing you ever saw."

"I wonder what happened to the pilot who came down in this?"

"Oh, him," Bandon said. "He's right over here." He led the way across the carpet of leaves under the giant trees to a thicket. "In there."

Chester parted the brush and looked into a bower of woven branches thatched with dried grass. On the dirt floor were three hand-made earthenware pots and a woven basket with the desiccated remains of what might have once been fruit. Beside the basket lay the skeleton of a man.

"Good Lord!" Chester muttered. "Poor devil."

"Can't figure what killed him—'less it was old age," Bandon said. "No arrows stickin' in him, no broken bones. Plenty of food and water, I'd say."

"He must have bailed out of his balloon, landed here and found himself marooned," Chester said. "But surely he could have signaled in some way . . ."

"Must have been a long time back—before our town was built. And there's no other Tricennium for twenty miles."

"What about the Center? It's not more than five miles."

"They just built that a year or two back. Nope, he was stuck, all right. Just like us. We might just as well hunker down beside him—"

"But why didn't he use the parachute? He could have rigged it somehow and jumped!"

Bandon eyed the sagging yellow-white cloth above. "Jump off the cliff with that trailin' behind him, hey? I dunno. I'd hate to try it."

Chester hitched up his belt. "You may just have to. Come on, let's get it down from there."

Chester and Bandon stood gazing sadly at the broad expanse of weather-spotted and puckered nylon stretched on the ground before them. Two long, dark tears in the material ran from edge to edge.

"I see why he didn't use it," Chester said glumly. "Well, that's that. The material's still sound, though. We might as well cut it up in sections for easy hauling and get back to work on our hut."

"Don't reckon we could sew it up," Bandon said doubtfully.

"Not a chance. We might manage to work some threads lose and lace it back together, but it wouldn't hold air. And with a double load—well, we'd splash when we hit."

Bandon winced. "Let's get busy. I'll salvage those pots and the basket. Must be water near here, 's the reason he camped here."

An hour later, having used Bandon's bone-handled hunting knife to dissect the parachute, Chester folded the sections, coiled the lines and settled down to wait for his companion's return. He could hear him crashing through nearby underbrush.

Bandon emerged, red-faced and scratched. "Found it," he said. "Little pothole, damn near buried in prickle bushes. We'll spend half our time just gettin' enough water to stay alive on."

"I'll use the hatchet to clear it away," Chester said. "Let's be going."

"Why not build right here?"

"I like the open glade near the edge better. Then, too, this place has certain morbid associations."

"You mean him?" Bandon nodded toward the dead man's hut. "Shucks, he can't hurt us."

"I'd like to be able to look out and see the rest of the world. Let's be moving. We have a lot to do before we can consider ourselves settled in."

"Squirrel food," Bandon said, spitting blackberry seeds. "Only three days on squirrel food, and my britches are so loose they'd fall off if I didn't have 'em roped on."

"Why don't you finish up that bow? Then maybe you'd be able to eat rabbit for a change," Chester said cheerfully. "Personally, I like berries."

"Bow's made," Bandon said shortly. "But I can't string it till I get a rabbit to gut. And I can't get a rabbit to gut till I—"

"Why don't you use nylon?"

"That stuff? Stretches like rubber. You couldn't throw an arrow fifty feet with that. And besides, I need arrowheads and feathers and glue. Now, I can make up a swell glue—just as soon's I can shoot a few critters."

"Chip some heads out of stone," Chester suggested. "And you ought to be able to find a few feathers around an old nest or some such place."

"I've got plenty of nice arrow shafts ready. Good tough, springy wood. And light."

Chester fingered an arrow. "You do nice work, Bandon. Too bad you left the part of the world where it would be appreciated. You could have fitted in nicely as an archery expert.''

''I wouldn't have been an archery expert if I hadn't thrown off the shackles first.''

''Still, if you go back . . .''

''Ha!'' Bandon looked out over the airy vista of distant ridges. ''Unless we turn into birds, that's not likely.''

Chester sat up suddenly, flexed the arrow shaft in both hands.

''Bandon, what kind of wood is that? Is there a good supply of it?''

Bandon raised an eyebrow at the excitement in Chester's tone. He waved a hand. ''The woods are full of it. What—''

''You say you can make glue?''

''Glue? Sure I can make glue. All you have to do is boil down a few carcasses . . .''

Chester was on his feet. ''Bandon, you get that bow of yours working. I don't care if you string it with shoelaces. Bring me in a brace of rabbits and boil up a pot of stickum.'' He picked up the hatchet, its blade bright now from use. ''I'm headed for the tall timber.''

''Hold on, here. What's goin' on? We've got plenty of firewood; and I've lost too much weight to go traipsin' off on a rabbit hunt.''

''For what I've got in mind, the lighter you are, the better. And I'm not hunting firewood; I'm after what they call aircraft spruce.''

''Chester, just what *have* you got in mind?''

''We're going to leave here, Bandon. It will take a few days, but we'll travel in style.''

''In style?''

"To be precise—in a home-built glider."

"She'll be built along the lines of an old-time training ship," Chester said. "Neat and simple."

"Simple? We've already got more junk lined up to go into this contraption than it would take to stock a store. Five kinds of wood, cloth, wire, string, glue—"

"And we're still grossly understocked, believe me. But I think we can do it."

"I don't see the need of usin' my knife to make that thing," Bandon said, watching Chester take long, curling shavings from a spruce spar with a jack plane made from a chunk of wood and the knife blade.

"It's a lot more efficient than a knife for trimming up structural members," Chester said. "How's the glue factory coming?"

"Oh, I've got enough glue to feather a million arrows. Can I quit boilin' down rabbit now and fix a couple to eat?"

"Sure. But don't overdo it. I wasn't kidding when I said the lighter we are, the better. Then I wish you'd go to work stripping down that clothesline; there's ten strands of steel wire under the plastic cover. We'll use that for diagonal frame-bracing. And I'll need lots of the nylon parachute lines unraveled, too. Reel it on a stick as you get it worked apart."

Bandon set to work. "I still don't see how you figure to flap the wings, Chester. To hold us up, you'll have to have a spread of maybe ten, twelve feet."

"Thirty," Chester said. "And a five-foot cord.

Not a very efficient layout, but I'm afraid it's the best we can do with the materials at hand. Figuring us each at one-fifty—or a little less, if we eat sparingly for another week—and the airframe at two hundred pounds, that works out to three pounds per square foot. And we won't flap our wings—unless I've miscalculated badly."

"Well, I guess you know what you're doin'."

"Certainly. In my youth I was a fanatical model-plane builder. Free-flight, control-line, RC, hand-launch—the works."

"You done much flyin' off cliffs?"

"Well, if you mean in full-scale aircraft—"

"I do."

"Actually, none."

"None? But you've built a lot of them, hey?"

"Well, not actually anything big enough to carry a man—but I did put together a seven-foot multi-engine control-liner."

"You mean we're goin' to jump over a cliff in a contraption you've never tried out before, and that you maybe don't know how to work even if it doesn't come apart?"

"The alternative," Chester pointed out, "is sitting up here in the eagle's nest until we get too old to pick berries."

Bandon shouldered his bow. "I'm goin' out and get us a couple of eatin' rabbits," he announced. "We might just as well eat and drink and enjoy it while we can."

"That's right," Chester said. "Because tomorrow—who knows?"

"It looks like a coffin for a tall, skinny corpse,"

Bandon said, eying the twenty-foot openwork structure of spruce strips propped on sawhorses made from peeled logs.

"Two tall, skinny fellow," Chester said. "You stretch out here." He indicated a section floored with woven strips of willow bark. "I take up the right-hand position beside you. I'll have to have room to edge forward or back to correct the trim. Now, I want you to go along wrapping each joint with nylon patches, and working in glue. What I wouldn't give for a few square feet of one-eighth birch ply and a pound or two of wire brads."

"While you're wishin', you might just as well wish for a concealed staircase leadin' from here into that air-conditioned restaurant you were talkin' about. You can have the blonde. Just leave me to the steaks and chops."

Chester jumped as a sudden *whop!* sounded behind him. He whirled. A long steel-tipped arrow quivered upright against the sod.

"They're shootin' at us," Bandon blurted. "Where are they?" He stared wildly around.

Chester swept the scene with a glance. "That arrow came straight down—and from not very high up." He pulled it from the ground. "It wasn't buried more than a few inches."

As Chester looked toward the cliff edge, a second arrow shot up into view, curved and fell twenty feet away.

"Ah-hah! They're pegging them up here with an arbalest of some sort." A moment later a round stone the size of a grapefruit sailed into view, slowed to a stop and dropped back out of sight. "They've got a catapult working, too. I hope that

161

drops back on someone's toe."

"I thought it was awful quiet these last few days," Bandon said. "They've been a busy bunch down there, gettin' ready to lay down a barrage on us."

Chester watched a second stone fly into view and drop with a thump fifty yards away. Other arrows nipped up; some fell back, others clattered to earth at distances from ten to a hundred feet.

"How do they know where to aim?" Chester asked. "They're hitting pretty close."

"There's a couple pairs of binoculars in the town," Bandon said. "I reckon a few of the skunks are staked out on the next ridge watchin' every move we make." He shook a fist in the presumed direction of the spies. "See if you can figure it out, blast you!" he yelled defiantly. He turned to Chester. "Maybe we'd better move 'er back to the edge of the woods."

"I don't think we're in any real danger, short of an accident," Chester replied, watching a rock clatter down thirty feet distant. "There are as many falling behind us as in front. Let's just keep at it and hope for the best. I wonder why they're so persistent? They should be content to let us starve up here in peace, one would think."

"It's not that easy," Bandon said. "Grizz can't afford to let me get away—or die off."

"Why not?"

"Well, I've been thinkin'. He doesn't know where the treasury is—and he's not the kind of fellow to forget a thing like that."

"Treasury? I hadn't heard about that before. What does it consist of, a hoard of salami, canned crackers and replacement tubes for the Tri-D?"

"Nope. Guns and powder, mostly."

"Hmmm. I was about to suggest that you might throw a note over the side giving directions to its location, but under the circumstances that would be unwise."

An arrow dropped five feet from the edge of the wing.

"Oh-oh. We can't have any punctures now that we've started covering. Bandon, maybe you'd better start a counter-barrage while I work on the gluing. When I need you to stretch the next panel, I'll call you."

"That's a mighty flimsy-looking thing." Bandon studied the nearly completed project. "How long before we have to try it?"

"Not long. There are the tail surfaces to cover and install and the controls to link up. I'd say by sundown we'll be about ready—but of course, the glue needs overnight to set up thoroughly."

"That tail's not very big." Bandon gestured toward the stabilizer and rudder frames propped against a tree. "Why not just leave 'em off?"

"Impractical, I'm afraid," Chester said. "No tail assembly, no flight. We'd drop like a stone— tail first."

Bandon jumped as a rock crashed down at his feet. "Maybe we'd better head for the tall brush before Grizz gets lucky," he suggested nervously.

"And let them knock the glider apart at their leisure? Not—"

With a crash, a four-inch stone slammed through the woven floorboards of the pilot's compartment. Chester stared at it in dismay.

11

A RUDDY DAWN was breaking over the distant eastern hills. Clutching an improvised cape about his shoulders against the early-morning chill, Chester examined the nylon-covered wing, glistening with dew.

"It looks as though she's survived the night intact."

"Here, look at this," Bandon called. He held up a paper-wrapped stone. "Looks like it might be a message." He stripped off the paper, glanced at it and handed it to Chester.

Kum don now and sav yerself frum gitin yer brans bust in. Bandon, it ant yu, jus the spi wer after. Grizz, bos.

"Well, that's an attractive offer," Chester said. "If you trust him."

Bandon snorted. "I heard him makin' promises to you a few days back. I reckon I'll take my chances with the flyin' machine. But, say, Chester, how do you figure on gettin' it over the edge? If we're both sittin' in it . . ."

"That's easy. We'll set up a pair of peeled willow rails; we'll use the poles we skinned for their bark. The glider will have to be anchored in position with a length of nylon line. When we're ready to go, I'll cut the cable. The rails will be laid up the slope at an angle, so a fifty-foot run ought to give us a good enough send-off. Of course, I'll have to put her nose down as soon as we're over the edge, to gain flying speed."

"Maybe if we rigged a weighted line and hung it over the edge, it would give her a little extra kick-off. We'd have to fix it so it'd drop off when we went over the edge."

"Good idea. You find us a suitable ballast stone—as big as you can lift. We'll try to get off before the morning barrage starts. I'll be ready to move her upslope and set up the track in about ten minutes."

Bandon nodded and moved off. Chester climbed into the pilot's compartment, stretched out face down and fitted his toes against the rudder bar. Looking over his shoulder, he could see the rudder wag in response to his foot movements. He tried the stick; the elevators flopped up and down correctly. A side pressure warped the trailing edge of the left wing panel up and down.

"Pre-flight check complete," Chester murmured to himself. He crawled out, moving carefully as the open-work fuselage creaked under his weight. Upslope, Bandon levered at a boulder with a pole. It lifted, teetered, started a slow trundle downhill.

"Bandon!" Chester called, running forward. "Stop that!"

166

Bandon stood frozen, watching the massive rock gather speed, aimed directly for the glider perched at the cliffside. Chester slid to a halt, turned and dashed back for the ship. He skidded around under the wing, seized the tail post and hauled. The glider slid back with a grate of wood against soil, then jammed—just as the boulder took a mighty bound and leaped over it to drop from sight over the cliff. Chester slumped against the frail craft.

"Hey, Chester, I'm sorry about that."

A mighty crash sounded from below, followed by faint yells. Chester went to the edge and looked over. A great gap showed in the mass of foliage far below. Through the opening Chester saw men darting about among the splintered remains of a wooden structure. Bandon arrived at his side and stared down silently.

"Well, blast those skunks, Chester. You see that? They were buildin' an almighty big catapult down there. See the throwin' arm layin' off there to the left? Pretty smart, hey, sneakin' around under cover of those trees and fixin' to let fly with the big stuff. By the nine tails of the hilldevil, it's a good thing that stone got away from me."

"Maybe—but I'd just as soon we didn't do anything so dramatic again. Let's get that track set up."

Chester studied the panorama. "We'll angle it to the right to avoid that depression near the edge. I'll aim her right off there between those two knolls. With luck, we can stretch our glide to half a mile. That ought to give us all the start we need on our welcoming committee."

"Wonder what's happened to the artillery this morning? I guess maybe that little pebble we dropped on 'em shook 'em up a little."

"I hope so. It would be a shame to suffer a hit now."

Chester and Bandon set to work pegging wooden rails in place. They finished, then took up positions on opposite sides of the craft and lifted it clear of the ground.

"Hey, it's not so heavy," Bandon commented.

"Watch your footing," Chester said.

Together they toiled up the slope, maneuvered carefully, then settled the ship in place on the track.

"Hold her while I chock her," Chester called. He wedged a sizable stone fragment in place under the down-tipped nose. "All right, now we rig the restraining cable."

Chester payed out a length of nylon to the nearest tree, tied it securely, then attached the other end to the keel of the glider between the two pilot positions.

"All set," he said, removing the chock from the track. "All that's holding her now is the cable. When I cut that—off we go."

"It sure is quiet," Bandon commented, looking around. "I wonder . . ."

"Let's just be grateful," Chester said. "I wasn't looking forward to having to launch right out through a hail of arrows. I'll lay out the ballast line now while you bring in a stone."

At the edge of the precipice, Chester dropped the coil of nylon line and tied a secure noose ready to receive the weighting stone. As he rose to turn back, an unshaven face rose into view not ten feet from him; two grimy hands scrabbled for a grip.

Chester jumped, put a foot square in the face and pushed. With a yelp, the man dropped back; a tremendous crash followed. Chester looked over the edge. Twenty feet below, a rickety platform thrust up; three men crouched atop it, while another sprawled on his back, half through the shattered decking. One of the three brought a bow into position and launched an arrow in one motion; it whistled past Chester's ear. He whirled, grabbed up a hundred-pound rock and eased it over the edge. There was a noisy crunch. Now two of the men clung frantically to the shattered remains of the platform, while the third scrambled agilely down the rickety structure. The fourth man was gone. Looking to the left Chester saw a second platform and beyond it a third. And there were more to the right.

Chester was up and running. "Bandon! Forget the stone! Get to the glider!"

Bandon stared, then dropped the rock and headed for the craft at a run. From the woods behind the glider a man in a soiled shirt and torn pants emerged, his bow at the ready. Bandon, in mid-stride, nocked an arrow and let fly. The new-comer fell backward, feathers at his throat.

"Into your seat, fast!" Chester yelled.

"Say, I'm not really sure I want to risk this," Bandon exclaimed.

At the cliff edge, two men came into view simultaneously, scrambling up, starting for the glider at a run. Bandon whipped his bow up, set an arrow, twanged it on its way, sped a second. One man whirled and fell; the other dived for cover. Bandon dropped the bow and slid into his place, face down. Chester jumped in after him, wriggled his feet up against the rudder bar. Reaching down with his right hand, he sawed at the tether with the knife blade. More men appeared. One raised a bow and let an arrow fly. It struck the nose block with a *whack*!, stood quivering in the wood. The rope parted. With a lurch, the little ship started forward, grinding and bumping along the green-wood tracks. Wind whistled in Chester's face. The running men had halted, staring. The bowman raised his bow, loosed an arrow, missed by yards. As the glider bore down on him, he turned and fled. More men were coming over the edge now.

"The skunks stayed up late last night plannin' this one," Bandon yelled in Chester's ear. "They—"

"Quiet!" Chester choked.

The glider seemed to move forward with infinite leisure. The grass and gravel moved past in a ribbon that blurred slowly. The cliff edge was ahead now, coming closer.

"We're not going to make it!" Chester mumbled. "Not enough speed."

An arrow slammed off the framework above Chester's head, knocking off splinters. Ahead was blue sky and distant, hazy hills.

"Now!" Chester gasped. Abruptly the grate of wood on wood ceased—and the bottom dropped from under them. Chester shoved forward on the stick convulsively, his breath caught in his throat, his heart slamming madly under his ribs. Down, down, falling, the wide spread of green rushing up, wind screaming now in the wires at Chester's side, buffeting his face. Lying prone, he pulled back on the stick, neutralizing it, then farther back . . .

He could feel the air pressure resisting the stick. He pulled harder, felt pressure build against his chest, saw the green below tilting away, flattening, saw the hills sliding down into view, with sky above them. He looked over the side. Treetops rushed past a hundred feet below.

"Hey!" Bandon yelled. "We're flyin', Chester!"

The nose rose, aiming now at the distant sky. Chester pushed the stick, felt the ship slow, hesitate minutely, then drop her nose. He swallowed. "Whip stall," he muttered. "Pilot-killers."

"Say, Chester, this is great!" Bandon called.

Chester inched forward, applied a little right rudder. The ship turned sloppily.

"A little aileron," Chester told himself. He edged the stick to one side, felt the ship tilt sharply. Air currents buffeted the glider. Chester gritted his teeth, fighting the motion. "Let it fly itself," he reminded himself, consciously relaxing. A gust rocked the craft; it righted itself. The nose crept up; Chester eased the stick forward. The nose came down. The flank of a hill was approaching. Chester applied rudder, co-ordinating the ailerons; the ship heeled, curved away.

"Wheeeee!" Bandon cried. "Just like a bird, Chester!"

There was a valley ahead, a steep cleft between hills. Chester aimed for it, holding a straight course. He drew a deep breath and let it out slowly.

"Nothin' to it, Chester," Bandon said. "Here, have some nuts."

"Not yet, thanks," Chester called. "For heaven's sake lie still and let me fly this thing."

"Say, Chester, that's funny," Bandon said.

"What's funny?"

"We're gettin' higher instead of comin' down. Hey, Chester, how are we goin' to get down if this thing keeps goin' up?"

"You're raving," Chester said.

Wind screamed past his face, making his eyes water. He twisted his head and looked over the side. The trees below were a smooth blanket of green. He looked back. The mesa was visible a mile away.

"You're right!" Chester said. "I can see the top of the mesa. I guess we've snagged a thermal!"

"Is that good or bad?"

"Good. Now don't bother me for a few minutes, and I'll see if I can stretch our glide to a new Tricennium record!"

"Five miles," Chester called. "That was the Center back there."

"What keeps her in the air, Chester, without flappin' her wings?"

"We're riding rising air currents off these slopes. We've got a very poor glide angle, I'm afraid, but the updrafts are so strong we're gaining altitude in spite of our inefficiency. I'm hoping to catch some true thermals over the plains ahead. I'd estimate our altitude at about three thousand feet now. I'd like to work her up to about five and then set out west toward the Tricennium of the Original Wisdom. If we can make a few miles it will save us a long, hot walk.''

"I'm all for it, Chester. I like it fine up here.''

"That remark seems to indicate you've abandoned your simple-life philosophy. An aircraft—even a primitive one like this—is a far cry from chipping flints.''

"Why, what do you mean, Chester? We made this ourselves, out of plain old wood and rabbit glue.''

"Plus a few bits of nylon and some steel wire. But after all, every manufactured item is made from simple raw materials—even a Tri-D tube. All materials are natural, if you trace them back to their beginnings. There's nothing wrong with rearranging nature to give ourselves a few more comforts—it's misusing what we make that takes the savor out of life.''

"Maybe so. But it's not really the *stuff*; it's the *people* that gravel me. I don't want anybody tellin' me what to do, tryin' to push me around. Soon's we land, I guess I'll head for the hills again.''

"Bandon, learn to do something that other people want or need and you won't have to worry about being stepped on. Most of the shrill cries of social injustice come from people who contribute nothing to the scene that a chimpanzee couldn't do better. Why do you think people treasure the few really talented singers, actors, ball players, medical men, engineers that crop up? Because there are far too few of them—every one is a treasure. And if a new man comes along and writes a song that reaches out and touches something in everybody, he doesn't have to worry about being picked on. His fans won't let anything happen to him.''

"Well, maybe I could start up an archery class, like you said. You suppose folks would come and want to learn?"

"Try it and find out. If there's something in archery that makes you love it, there'll be others that will get the same thrill. Be best at something—and let the world know it."

"Hey, Chester, look down there. A line running right across the countryside."

"A road," Chester explained. "That's good. We can follow it right back to town."

"And way up ahead—looks like buildings, away off."

"That's possible. From this altitude, the Tricennium should be visible; it's only about fifteen miles."

Chester squinted overhead for cumulus clouds, steered for the shadow of the nearest. The updraft rocked the tiny craft. "All right, Bandon, here we go." He banked the glider to the right and struck out for the distant city.

Half an hour later the glider whistled in past a row of tall trees, cleared an outlying house by inches, settled in over a broad green lawn. It skimmed for a hundred yards, then dropped with a mild jar to skid for another fifty feet before heeling over with one wing tip scooping up turf, describing an abrupt arc and coming to rest.

"Whew!" Chester sighed. He rose to hands and knees and looked around at the well-manicured greenery, the peaceful rooflines and the half-dozen men coming across the lawn at a job trot.

"Get ready for a rude reception, Bandon. I'm

not certain these fellows quite appreciate *my* little contribution to society. They may be the pushy kind.''

''Well, I'd like to see 'em try it with me,'' Bandon growled.

''Don't leap to any untenable conclusions: they're a mild-looking lot, but they're full of surprises.''

The leading greeter came up. ''Extraordinary!'' he commented, looking at the glider, Chester, Bandon and the long groove in the velvety lawn. ''Where in the world did you come from?''

A second man came up. ''Now, Gayme, what did I tell you? A stiff-winged, manned aircraft. Look at these two chaps. As ordinary a pair as you'd care to meet. So much for your talk of the supernormal.''

''The manifestation is, I insist, supernormal, in the sense that it surpasses the ordinary run of events. Note the lack of motive power. How did such an assemblage of artifacts and personnel come to be up there to begin with?''

''Look here,'' Chester said.

''Tut, tut, Gayme. I'm sure there's a simple, rational explanation. I suggest we start at the beginning by asking a few questions.'' He eyed Bandon. ''You, sir. Do you mind telling me just how you came to descend from an empty sky?''

''Sure, easy,'' Bandon said. ''I live on a cloud, and I just came down to get a refill on moonbeams. Any other questions? If not, how about a few eats? I'm hungry.''

''Ah-hah,'' Gayme crowed. ''Just as I suspected. We'll consult Norgo.''

"This is where I came in," Chester said. "Look, Bandon, I'll just slip over to the town square and see to a few things. I may not see you again. If I don't, I hereby will you full rights to the glider. Don't let them euchre you out of it; they're good at appropriating things in the name of science. And work on your archery."

"Hold on, Chester. Say, I figure we get on pretty good together. I figured you and I'd stick together."

"Sorry, Bandon, old chap. It's been a most rewarding experience, but I have some unfinished business to attend to—if it isn't altogether too late. I'm going to find an inconspicuous corner and lie low for a few hours. Good luck."

Bandon took his hand. "Well, all right, Chester. Sorry about gettin' you into that fix back there."

"Thus," Gayme droned on, "the phenomenon is related to the spontaneous precipitation of frogs sometimes reported from outlying areas."

"Who is outlying whom?" his friend inquired archly. "Now, I . . ."

Chester moved off quietly across the lawn. No one called after him.

In gathering twilight Chester moved across the square toward the shadows of the cupola, the scene of his arrival ten months earlier. As he reached the flower bed ringing the monument, a tall figure stepped before him, peered at Chester's lithe, broad-shouldered figure, his tanned face, sinewy arms, short-clipped sun-bleached hair and tight-fitting Tricennium costume.

"Oh, sorry," he said. "I was waiting for the poor little nincompoop who had the fixation regarding the rug. They say he slipped away from the Center right in the middle of the experiment. You're one of Norgo's crew?''

''I'm the poor little nincompoop,'' Chester said flatly. ''Get out of my way, Devant.''

''Wha . . . ? Is it really you?''

''It's really me—and I'm reclaiming my property now.''

Devant laughed. ''Still the same pathetic line, eh? Well, Norgo warned that you'd probably head for here. I'll take you back now to finish your course of experimental study.''

''I graduated.''

''Oh, really?'' Devant laughed again easily, reached for Chester. There was a brief flurry of motion and Devant hit the pavement—hard.

''Glad I ran into you, Devant,'' Chester said, stepping over him. ''That's one piece of unfinished business out of the way. If I find I'm too late to help my friends, I'll be back to finish the job.''

Devant scrambled up with a shout. There were answering calls, the pad of running feet. Chester sprinted for the rug, veered around a stone bench, made out the dim outline of a chair. An overhead light glared suddenly, showing Chester a ring of men closing in, Norgo in the lead, holding up a hand. The posse halted.

''Computer, are you there?'' Chester called urgently. There was a long pause.

''Chester, you know you aren't allowed on the rug,'' Norgo called. ''Just come along quietly now.''

''Watch him,'' Devant cautioned, dabbing at his cheek. ''He's learned a few tricks.''

"Ah, Mr. Chester"—the familiar voice spoke from midair—"I had a little difficulty in locating you."

"Stand by," Chester said. "I'll be with you in a moment." He turned to face Norgo. "I'm sorry to rush off," he called, feet planted on the rug. "I'd have enjoyed staying longer, but personal affairs demand my attention. Give my regards to Kuve—and watch out for a rabble-rouser named Grizz. He lives up in the hills, but he's planning on moving into town soon."

"I had hoped your delirium would clear up once you were separated from your fetish object," Norgo said sadly. "Too bad." He signaled; the posse closed in.

"Goodbye, Norgo," Chester called. "Thanks for everything. And after I'm gone, remember: accept reality. Is-not is not not-is.

"All right, Computer," he added, "take me back to Genie."

12

MISTY TWILIGHT turned to the glare of day on a city street. Chester looked around. Nothing had changed from his last glimpse of the scene ten months before, except that the crowd had dwindled to a few diehards. The street was still roped off, although the phalanx of squad cars had been reduced to two vehicles, each with a pair of heavyweights in the front seat, none of whom was looking his way.

"Don't go away, Computer," Chester said softly. "I'll have to try to find Genie, and it may take a while."

"Very well, Mr. Chester," the computer's voice replied loudly. "I'll occupy myself with an analysis of—"

"Quiet!" Chester snapped, too late. Four round cop faces turned to stare at Chester. Car doors swung open; flat feet scrambled. Two cops advanced on Chester while two more rounded their vehicles, hitching at red leather pistol belts.

"Hey, what's them chairs and rug doin' back here?" one cop demanded.

"Who're you, Bud?" another spoke up.

Chester folded his arms and glared at the lead cop. "I thought I left instructions that this area was to be watched closely," he barked. "Who dumped these things here? You men think this is a used-furniture store?"

"What's that?" the lead cop said, letting his mouth hang open.

"Button your coat," Chester snapped. "And see that you shave before coming on duty next time." He put his hands behind his back and strode along the line of cops. "Sergeant, those boots need attention. And your car needs a wash."

"Hey, who're you?" a cop said.

"Who're you, *sir*!" Chester roared. "Don't you know the field uniform of a Commissioner of Police when you see one?"

"Sure," the cop replied promptly. "And that ain't it."

"State Police, that is," Chester amended.

"State Police? Heck, I seen the State Police Commissioner at the race track just last week."

"State *Department* Police, you nincompoop!" Chester bellowed. "Don't you men realize this is a matter of international import? Why," he went on in a confidential tone, "I have it on good authority that the affair ties in with a scheduled interplanetary invasion."

"Geez," a cop said.

"Now," Chester went on smoothly, "do you men happen to recall the case of the unclothed young woman who was arrested in this vicinity some time ago?''

The cops looked at each other. One lifted his chrome-plated helmet and squinted upward.

''Well,'' he said. ''Ahhh . . .''

''I *think* maybe I remember something about that,'' another cop volunteered.

''Ah, fine. Can you tell me what disposition was made of the case? It seems to have slipped my memory.''

''Well, let's see . . .''

''Perhaps she served a brief sentence and was sent on her way,'' Chester suggested. ''She might even have gotten a job—somewhere nearby.''

''A job,'' a cop repeated, staring at Chester.

''Why don't you come on down to the station house . . . ah . . . Commissioner? Maybe we can fix you up down there.''

''Why, she may still be right there in the women's cell block,'' another cop spoke up. ''Maybe you can have a nice little visit with her.''

''An excellent suggestion, men,'' Chester said crisply. ''You may drive me down at once.''

''Sure. Right this way.''

Chester followed two of the officers to their car. He rode along in silence, turning over ways and means. It was unlikely that after ten months Genie was still in the local lockup. Still, she might have compounded the original offense by assaulting members of the police force, damaging public property, attempting escape, resisting arrest and failing to produce a driver's license. And, of course, she was penniless—always a disadvantage when reasoning with the law.

The car drew up to a side entrance to a red brick building with twin pillars surmounted by milky white globes lettered POLICE. Chester stepped out and followed the driver up the steps while his partner trailed. Inside, the cop motioned Chester along a short corridor and into an inner room where a thin man in a red uniform glanced up from behind a desk with an irritated expression.

"Okay, Buddy," the lead cop said, looking at Chester. "Look who we got here—the International Commissioner of Police. Get a load of the outfit."

"Now, I'd like to know—" Chester started, stepping foward.

"He shows up in the stakeout and wants to know do we remember the dame we picked up down there."

"And by the way, the chairs and rug are back," the other cop volunteered.

The man behind the desk jumped up. "Back, are they? Did you get whoever delivered them?"

"And he says it's an invasion from Mars," the cop finished. "Naw, they was too quick for us. They had this fast car, see—"

"You imbeciles! Kablitzki, I'll have your stripes for this! Now get back down there and keep that area under surveillance—and that doesn't mean sitting in your car listening to the latest jerk-and-twitch record!"

"But, Chief, what about our pinch here? He's a dangerous nut case."

The Chief threw a glance at Chester. "Probably

an escapee from a TV commercial. Lock him up for obstructing justice.''

"Look here—'' Chester began.

The two cops turned to him with expressions of relief, reaching out large square hands. Chester leaned aside, caught an outstretched arm, flipped the hand back and applied pressure. The cop yowled and leaped, landed in a heap.

"I simply want some information," Chester declared. "The girl I asked about—is she still under confinement?"

The second cop growled and moved in. Chester stiff-handed him under the third button, clipped him on the side of the neck as he fell past.

"Here—'' the Chief cried, reaching for a drawer. Chester was across the desk, his hands gripping the thin man's collar.

"Listen, you confounded idiot!" Chester barked. "Where is the girl—the one you picked up for indecent exposure?"

The Chief struggled manfully; Chester rapped his head against the floor. One of the cops staggered into view. Chester hit him with the Chief.

"Now look," he insisted, holding the unfortunate official in an awkward position over the back of his padded chair. "All I want is information on the young lady's whereabouts. Why not cooperate in giving a little help to a law-abiding citizen?"

"She's . . . in the women's wing—north side, first cell on the right."

"Where are the keys?"

"It's a . . . combination."

"What's the combination?"

The office door burst open. A fat cop goggled, tugged at a heavy pistol in a hip holster. Chester swung the Chief around as a shield. More cops appeared. In the corridor a bell clanged stridently. Feet pounded. Chester hurled the Chief from him, turned, crossed his arms over his face and dived through the wide double-hung window, landed on grass in a tinkle of glass shards, rolled and came up running. He leaped the hedge, heading for a dark alley mouth across the street. A man stepped into his path.

"Don't let 'em get away," Chester bawled. The man stepped aside, looking startled. Chester sprinted up the alley, emerged in a busy street, fell back to a brisk walk. The coup had been a failure, but at least he knew where Genie was. Poor girl! Almost a year in a cold, gray cell.

In the next block Chester skidded to a halt before a wide plate-glass window against which six-inch letters spelled out CATERPILLAR MOTORS. Beyond the glass crouched a giant yellow vehicle, aglitter with chrome, spotlights, aerials. A placard before the looming golden monster said:

THE NEW CATERPILLAR CONVERTIBLE FOR '67
(White Sidewall Tracks Extra)

There was an inconspicuous door beside the picture window. Chester pushed it open. Inside, a man with greased hair and a smile leaned against the polished flank of the mighty machine, talking to a paunchy customer of middle age.

". . . convenient monthly payments," he was saying. Chester eased behind the immense convertible, climbed softly up, opened the bubble canopy and settled himself in the yellow leather seat. Gleaming instruments winked up at him from a polished panel. Down below the salesman said, ". . . heat and music, window washers, backup lights, power seats, windows, top, steering, brakes, clasho-mesh transmission, triple tank-drain carburetion, luxurious cardboard interior, garbage disposal, foam-rubber mats, TV screen. . ."

Chester looked over the panel, located the starter. ". . . jet-blast mufflers," the salesman was saying. "Not one but—get this—two, yes, *two* Last Trump air horns, a full complement of cheery flashing lights in place of tiresome dials . . ." Chester switched on, pressed the starter. The engine caught with a roar. He shifted into low, moved toward the show window. The startled salesman yelled and leaped clear; the customer scuttled for safety. The great polished blade hit the glass, sent it clattering in jagged shards. The convertible rumbled through the opening, pivoted to the right, bounced a diminutive passenger car aside, took the center of the avenue. Chester sounded the Last Trump horns as the clasho-mesh shifted into high with a squeal of treads. The crowd scattered before the onrushing monster. An alert patrol car started up, gunned back into the car's path. Chester swerved, felt the rear quarters of the smaller vehicle crunch as the treads mounted it. He swerved to avoid a Good Humor man, clipped a beer truck with the tip of the blade, dumping it on its side. A head formed in the street.

Chester rounded into the street where a scattering of excited office workers clustered on the courthouse lawn. The north wing, the Chief had said. Chester squinted at the sun, steering for the opening in the hedge. North was to the right.

People were staring, pointing, then turning to run as the giant machine clattered across the curb, trampled the hedge and struck out across the lawn. A petunia bed disappeared under the relentless treads. High in the red brick side of the building, narrow barred windows were set at ten-foot intervals. Beneath them, the caterpillar ground to a halt. Over the rumble of the engine Chester heard excited cries. Faces appeared at the cell windows.

Chester opened the cab door and leaned out. "Genie!" he called. "It's I, Chester!"

There was a boom, and a bullet whined off the flank of the convertible. Chester ducked back inside. Above, he saw a familiar oval face appear at a window. He waved frantically. Genie waved back uncertainly. Chester threw the clasho-mesh in reverse and gunned back, pivoted, then moved forward. He set the corner of the blade against the brick wall and pressed the accelerator. The treads ground; the caterpillar bucked, then the treads spun helplessly as the turf gave way. A mighty stream of soil boiled out behind the machine.

Chester backed, lowered the blade, then raced the engine. The massive machine leaped forward and crashed against the brick wall with a thunderous impact. Chester felt the seat lurch; then bricks and mortar were falling, bounding off the polished hood, clattering against the plastic canopy. Clouds of dust rose. Timbers dropped, bent nails showing, where broken two-by-four studding dangled.

Chester backed off, looked over the situation. The gun boomed again, four times, rapidly. Two stars appeared in the plastic dome near his head. The cell-block wall showed a six-foot-high, ten-foot-wide gap, through which office furiture was visible. As he watched, another section of mortared bricks dropped. He moved in, hit the wall again. When he backed out from the load of debris, the upper floor joists were visible, sagging under a horizontal steel member. Chester moved in, jarred the wall again. A large section fell, exposing the open sides of two cells. He could see the iron-legged cots aslant on the tilted floor.

Chester maneuvered the caterpillar close to the shattered wall, raised the canopy and shouted to Genie. She appeared, on hands and knees, looking down over the edge at the huge, rumbling machine.

"Come on, quickly, Genie!" Chester beckoned urgently. He took a look over his shoulder. The fat cop was struggling to stuff cartridges into the cylinder of his foot-long revolver. Other cops were running in various directions.

"Is it really you, Chester?" Genie's voice quavered.

"Hurry!" Chester held up his arms. Genie moved then, turning to lower her trim, booted legs over the side, then slide down, hang by her hands and drop. Chester caught her, bundled her inside and slammed down the bubbletop just as the cop's gun went off. He backed quickly, turned, gunned off across the lawn. There were more shots. A bullet clanged off the canopy.

"Chester—it *is* you! You look so different—so handsome!"

"Genie, I'm sorry. I didn't mean to run out on you; I got back as soon as I could. But—"

"Why, Chester, you were marvelous! I knew it was you as soon as you said 'it is I' instead of 'it's me.' Wherever did you get this marvelous machine?"

"Nice, isn't it? Just the thing for traffic. Air conditioning, soundproofing—and bulletproof glass, luckily for us. But what I wanted to say was, I'm terribly sorry about you having to spend almost a year in jail."

"A year? Why, Chester, it hasn't been more than two hours since the policemen took us away!"

Chester blinked. "But . . . but . . ."

"Where will we go now, Chester? And where did you get those clothes, and that suntan, and those big, strong arms?"

"I . . . but I mean—you . . . Well, never mind. We'll figure it out later. Right now we have to clear a path through to the rug."

Chester swung the caterpillar into the street where the cop-guarded rug waited. A fire engine, approaching at flank speed, swerved, mounted the curb, clipped off a fire plug and came to a halt in a striking display of waterworks. Chester slowed, crimped the wheel, lumbered past a police car and crunched to a stop. He opened the canopy and, amid shouts, assisted Genie out. She leaped lightly across the remains of splintered yellow sawhorses to the rug. Chester followed. A pair of the ever-

present pink-coated policemen charged, sticks
ready.

"Now!" Chester said, seizing Genie's hand.
"Take us back to where we left Case, Computer!
And don't make any mistakes on your co-
ordinates this time!"

13

THE SHADOWS of the tall buildings dissolved into sunny skies. Chester and Genie stood on the grassy slope in the shade of the spreading branches. She turned to him, put soft arms around him.

"Oh, Chester. This is such fun!"

"Fun? Great heavens, Genie! Those people were shooting real bullets at us!"

"But you wouldn't let anything happen, I know."

"Well—at least it's a great relief to know you didn't actually spend a year in that cell. If you knew how I've been picturing you, languishing in durance vile—and Case! I assumed I was far too late to help him—but now, if we hurry—"

"I'm sure he'll be all right." Genie looked anxiously toward the ridge. "Still, I don't see the smoke any longer. I hope the fire hasn't burned down to the proper size for Mr. Mulvihill already."

"If those blasted natives have singed one hair of Case's head, I'll mow the whole tribe down!"

Twenty minutes' brisk walk brought them to the edge of the forest. On the trail ahead, two clean-shaven, sarong-clad men and a beautifully proportioned woman appeared. They paused, then flung up hands in greeting and began to dance and sing.

"Looks like a different tribe," Chester said. "Much better-looking people."

"They seem to want us to follow them."

With excited beckoning gestures the natives had turned and were darting away along a path.

"Well, we happen to be going in that direction anyway."

Chester and Genie moved on along the rough trail, came to the clearing where they had watched Case battle the giant.

"Not a sign of them," said Chester, looking around. "The cages are gone, everything." They pressed on, climbed a wooded slope and emerged from the forest into a wide village street, tree-lined and shady, bordered by beds of wild flowers behind which neat huts of brick, boards or split saplings dotted a parklike lawn. From a large house halfway along the street an imposing old man emerged, clad in neatly cut shorts and vest of coarse cloth. He pulled at a vast white beard as he came toward them.

"Good Lord!" said Chester, bewildered. "This is the wrong place, Genie! What kind of setting have you landed us in this time?"

"I don't know, Chester."

"Look at the old man with the beard. He's immense. I'll swear he must be an early Mulvihill; he looks enough like Case to be his grandfather.''

The old man came up, looked piercingly at Chester, then at Genie. He pulled at his beard, nodding to himself.

"Well," he said. "So you came back after all."

Chester and Genie sat with Case on benches under a wild-cherry tree at the crest of a rise that fell away to a blue lake under steep pine-covered hills. A native girl poured brown wine from a stone jar into irregular mugs of heavy glass.

"Tell me that again, slow and easy, Chester," said Case. "You say it's the same day as when you left here?"

"For Genie it is. I lived through ten months."

"You *do* look different, Chester. I guess there's more to this business than meets the eye. That damn computer must have its time meters scrambled."

"Case, we thought they'd be roasting you alive. How did you manage to get into their good graces?"

"Well, let's see. The last I saw of you two, you were sneaking off behind a tree. I kept juggling for an hour. Then I did a few back flips and handstands, and then I got them to give me a rope and rigged it and did some rope-walking. By that time they'd noticed you were gone. I made a few motions to give 'em the idea you'd flown away in good demon style. They didn't care much; they wanted to see more rope work."

"By that time you must have thought we'd abandoned you."

"I admit I was a little mad at first when you

didn't come charging over the hill with the Marines in tow. I guess it took a couple of years to get used to the idea I was stuck here. I figured something had happened to you, and I'd better just make the best of it. By that time I rated pretty high with the locals. They let me have the best den back in the thicket, and brought me all the food I wanted. It wasn't fancy but it was an easy life. Course, after thirty years . . .''

''Thirty years!''

Case nodded his white-maned head. ''Yep. Near as I can tell. I used to cut notches in a tree for the years, but sometimes I was so busy I forgot.''

''Busy? Doing what?''

''Well, there I was laying around all day, doing nothing, watching the natives scratch for a living, dirty, hungry, ignorant, dying of diseases, getting chewed up by bears or wildcats. And the food they gave me—half-raw dog meat, pounded raw turnips, now and then a mess of sour berries. Every now and then I'd have to put on a show, a little juggling or acrobatic work, just enough to keep the evil spirits out of town.

''Then one day I got to thinking. The country around here was the kind of real estate some smart developer could make a fortune out of back home. All it needed was the brush cut back and the trees trimmed and the lake shore cleaned up and garbage piles carted off somewhere and some fruit trees and flowers planted . . .

''Well, before I could do any tree-trimming I had to have an ax. That meant I needed some iron. By that time I could get by O.K. in the native language. I asked 'em if they knew any place where

there was red dirt; told 'em it was important magic.
A few weeks later a hunting party came back from
the other side of the lake with some pretty good
samples. The witch doctor had some coal—used it
to carve gods out of, 'cause it was easy to work. I
built a furnace and piled it full of lumps of ore and
chunks of coal and set it off, and, sure enough,
after a couple of hours melted iron started running
out the bottom of the furnace."

"Case, what do you know about smelting
iron?" Chester interrupted. "You didn't happen to
bring along *The Handyman's Home Smelter's
Handbook,* did you?"

"I cast half a dozen ax and hatchet heads in clay
molds the first time. They came out pretty good. I
sharpened 'em up on a flat stone, and then heated
'em and dunked 'em in a pot of water. They hard-
ened pretty good. Later on I got the formula down
pat. It depends mostly on how much coal and stuff
you've got in with the ore."

"A carbon content of between .7 and 1.7 per
cent produces the optimum combination of hard-
ness and malleability," said Genie.

"I wish you'd been here, kid," said Case with a
sigh. "You could have been a big help. But we
managed. I pounded out a knife blade and fitted a
handle to it and used that to cut ax handles. Then I
put the natives to work clearing land—and it wasn't
for show. The local wild life couldn't sneak up on the
village any more—no cover. I had 'em root out all
the bushes and coarse stuff, and the native grasses
took over. We undercut all the trees as high as a man
could reach. Then I had 'em shape the trees, pull
down all the vines and stuff. Made it look like a

regular park around here.

"Then we went to work on the lake. We made up some flat boats and got out and cleaned up the dead branches and cattails and then did a little dredging; built up a nice beach along this side. I rigged some fishing gear out of leather strips, showed 'em how to catch trout, and then staged a big fish fry. They didn't want to touch the fish; wasn't what their grandpaws ate, I guess. These kids were as conservative as a bunch of Ivy League alumni. But I gave 'em the old magic routine and they tried it. Now they spend half their time out on the lake. We made up a couple of saws and I showed 'em how to slice a tree into boards, and we built a few rowboats. Funny thing was, before long a couple of boys were ahead of me on boat-building—and fishing too. I made 'em up some bows and arrows and cast some iron arrowheads. Made up skinning knives and showed 'em how to scrape a hide and work it till it was soft.

"There were a lot of wild sheep and cattle around. We made up a batch of braided ropes and went out and brought in a couple of young goats and a half-grown critter that looked like an overgrown Texas longhorn. Later on we got a couple of newborn calves, a male and a female. In a couple of years we had a nice herd going. We let 'em graze the park here to keep the grass down. And o' course I showed 'em how to milk, and we experimented around and made some cheese."

"I didn't know you knew that much about animal husbandry," Chester put in.

"Anybody that's worked around a circus knows which end of a critter to feed. That was the least of my problems. I was getting a lot of pleasure out of admiring the beach and the park, and thinking what a pile of dough I could make out of it if I had it all back home. Then I'd see a couple of the local gals come trotting by, buck naked, grimy, fat, with stringy hair, and pretty gamy, if you got too close to 'em.'' Case sighed. ''I wasn't much better, I guess. I'd kinda got out of the habit of shaving, and there wasn't too much point in taking a bath if you had to put the same old leather drawers back on. So I decided it was time to give a little thought to developing the feminine industries.

''The first thing I needed was some cloth, to get away from the smell of hides. I tried some wool off these goats we keep. It wasn't much good. We scouted around for some wild cotton, but couldn't find any. Finally discovered a kind of flax. Went to work and rigged up a spinning wheel. That took the best part of a year, but we finally worked it out. We spun up a big batch of yarn. I had a loom ready; that wasn't so hard. We set it up and wove us a blanket.

''Well, I trained a few of the girls, and set 'em to work spinning and weaving. Made up some needles out of bone; couldn't manage it in steel. I wasn't much of a seamster, but I had lots of time. I cobbled up a pair of breeches for myself first, then a shirt. But heck, it's too warm here for sleeves, and anyway they're hard to make. I settled on a vest; it's just right to keep the chill off on a cool morning.''

''What about the winter?''

''Funny thing, there don't seem to be any seasons here. Stays about like this year around.''

"Pre-Ice Age," Genie murmured.

"Then I had to make soap. I messed around with animal fat and ashes and finally worked out a pretty good formula. I had to make 'em wash, at first, but I gave 'em the old Great Spirit routine, and pretty soon they were down at the lake scrubbing something every time I turned around. They're as bad as a bunch of Methodists when it comes to trying to make points upstairs with something easier than laying off sin. And once you get clean, you itch if you start letting dirt pile up again—and you start noticing your roommate—so the last few holdouts got dunked and scrubbed.

"Then I saw the need for a little civic improvement. The dump where we'd been living all this time was alive with fleas and rats and the damnedest collection of chewed bones, worn-out hides, magic frogs' innards, mummified totem animals, and other junk—just like Grandma's attic back home. They were a little mad at first when I burned it down. I told 'em it was the word from on high and that the place had to go, but there was a crafty little devil of a witch doctor that had the confounded gall to stand up and call me a liar. Imagine!''

"Well, after all, Case, you had been telling them everything you'd been doing was divinely ordained."

"Worked pretty good, too. It might even be true. Anyway, after I took the witch doctor down and dumped him in the lake, nobody else complained."

"You were lucky he let it go at that. From what I've read about shamans, they can be dangerous enemies."

"Oh, I hadn't taught anybody to swim yet."

"You mean you drowned him? Case, wasn't that a little drastic?"

"Maybe. But I figured that if I was setting up a society, I might as well do it along realistic lines. There's no point in letting somebody half your size push you around—especially when you're right. A weakling makes as bad a dictator as anybody else. The way I saw it, it was up to me to stand up for my ideas."

"The next big man might not be as interested in the public welfare as you were, Case. What then?"

"To tell you the truth, Chester, I wasn't interested in the public welfare. I was only interested in making a comfortable place for me to live in. I wanted clean, healthy people around, because I don't like smelling dirty, sick ones. I wanted them to live good so they'd have the time and inclination to learn the things I was trying to teach them, like fishing—so I could eat fish; raising beef, so I could eat steak—and, later on, painting pictures that I could look at and making music for me to hear and taking an interest in cookery so they could lay on a good feed for me and being happy so there'd be a nice atmosphere in the village. In the end I discovered that I got a lot more pleasure out of associating with a nice bunch of people than out of anything else.

"I started some of 'em wood-carving, and other ones farming, and some of them making glass. I scoured the woods for new plants we could raise for food, and I kept trying out new dirt samples for other metals. Now we've got copper and lead and a little gold—and I've trained people to go on looking. I've started 'em thinking about things and trying new ideas. And ever since I drowned the witch doctor, I've played down the spirit angle. The younger generation doesn't need the threat of spooks to do things; they've got an interest that keeps them busy. A lot of them are way ahead of me now. They learn fast. I wouldn't be surprised if one of 'em doesn't invent chemistry any day now, or fire up a steam engine, or discover medicine.''

"But a tyrant . . ."

"Any tyrant that sets up shop around here better be damned sure he doesn't develop any unpopular tastes," said Case. "These folks put up with me because I bring 'em good things. They're selfish, just like me. I've established a precedent. The next boss better keep it up, or he'll be joining the witch doctor.''

"It seems to have worked out well," Chester said, looking around at the peaceful village in the gathering twilight. "Still, I can't help feeling you should have instilled a little more idealism in them. Suppose they fall on hard times? What if the climate changes, or an epidemic strikes, or even a forest fire?''

"I don't think phony idealism would help. As far as I can see, all these schemes to make people squeeze into somebody's Grand Plan for Elevating Humanity usually end up with the elevatees on the short end of the stick. Everybody has his place in this village and a job to do that he's good at. My shoemakers can hold their heads up and the same goes for the fishermen and the hunters and the miners and the weavers and the vintners and the potmakers.''

"What about the arts? With this materialistic orientation . . ."

"Everybody dances and everybody sings. They all play games and they all make statues out of mud and they all paint. Some are better than others, but it's doing it that counts. In our setup everybody's an artist, not just a few half-cracked far-outers.''

"There don't seem to be many people here,'' said Genie. "Not more than three hundred, I'd estimate.''

"Too many people in one place mean problems. Sanitation, transportation, noise, conflict of interests. There's plenty of wide-open real estate. I've got twelve other villages going within fifty miles of here—and none of them have over three hundred people. Everybody can have all the kids they want, but if you put the village over the three-hundred mark, off you go to start your own. There's always plenty of volunteers to go along—people that want to get a good spot right on a lake or river, or hunters that like the idea of a virgin territory. There's a lot of trade among the towns, and the men usually get their wives from another village. Seems like it's human nature to prefer to go to bed with a stranger.''

"It makes the Internal Revenue Bureau seem very remote,'' Chester said. "Why do we surround outselves with unnecessary complexities?''

"Chester, this is a pretty good place here. Why don't you just settle down and forget all that?''

Chester shook his head. "I started off by trying

to wiggle out of my tax problem with illegal schemes to make money. Then, when I landed you in trouble, I sneaked away and left you.''

''But we agreed—''

''Genie tried to help me, and I left her stranded, too,'' Chester went on. ''I'd just about hit bottom when Kuve took me in hand. When I broke out of the Research Center, I made up my mind I'd settle my score. I helped out a fellow named Bandon, and I paid Devant for a couple of undignified incidents. Then I was lucky enough to find Genie. I'm sorry about your tough time, Case. I've cost you thirty years.''

''Best thirty years of my life, Chester. And now you're even.''

''No, I still have the circus to think about.''

''Hey, that's right, Chester. If it's really thirty years ago—I mean if thirty years haven't gone by—then maybe it's not too late to salvage something yet!''

''And,'' Chester went on, ''there's Great-grandfather's invention to see to. He spent his life on it—and he's left it in my hands. It's up to me to save it. And there's something else, too.''

Case got to his feet. ''Well, no time like the present, Chester. Let's get going.''

Half an hour later, Chester, Case, Genie and a chattering group of villagers stepped under the trees toward the rug and the two brocaded chairs.

''Case, I suppose you'll want to make a speech, appoint a successor, make a few prophecies, whatever white gods usually do before sailing off into the sunset.''

Case sighed. ''I've got a lot of friends here,

Chester. I'll hate to leave 'em. But there's no point in making a national holiday out of it. I've been trying to teach 'em how to run things for thirty years. I don't guess any last-minute instructions are going to change anything."

"Then let's go, Genie," Chester said. "But be sure you put us back in the right spot: specifically, Great-grandfather's underground control room."

Genie had a faraway look in her eyes. "I'm in touch with the computer," she said. "But . .."

"What is it, Genie?"

"It appears," she said, "that the world we started from no longer exists."

14

"A NUMBER OF AWFUL suspicions are beginning to crystalize into convictions," Chester said. "Your villages, with their population limit of three hundred, and the Tricennia, where I spent a year. Could that have been *this* society at some remote time in the future?"

"Beats me, Chester. I've given up trying to figure out anything that has to do with that blasted computer."

"If so, that would mean we've tampered with actual reality. We asked the computer to show us scenes of the past in the simplest possible way—"

"You mean that infernal contraption came up with the genuine article instead of a good honest fake?"

Chester nodded. "I'm afraid our hoax has backfired, Case. The computer really is a time machine."

"When we were bodily transferred into the past," Chester said, "our presence there altered the future. I recall now that the computer seemed to imagine that the Tricennium was Great-grandfather's basement.''

''But what about the city with those awful pink policemen, Chester?'' Genie asked. ''It was very similar to home, except for being a little out of date—and I imagine that was because Mr. Mulvihill's absence unbalanced things a little.''

''Case had only been here a short time then; he hadn't yet altered things completely out of recognizable shape.''

''So I guess we settle here after all.''

''Let's ask the computer a few questions. Are we completely cut off from getting back home, Genie?''

''A wide spectrum of entropic streams was rendered invalid by factors at the eighth level of complexity stemming from Mr. Mulvhill's introduction . . .''

''Yeah,'' Case cut in, ''but what about Chester's estate?''

''It has been relegated to the status of an unrealized pseudo-reality.''

''Why didn't that moronic aggregation of war-surplus parts mention this in the first place?''

''It's a machine, remember,'' Chester said. ''No initiative. We didn't ask.''

''Well, if the house is gone, then where's the computer?''

''Shunted to a temporal vacuole,'' Genie said.

''Hey, Chester,'' Case said. ''I've got a crafty notion.'' He raised his voice. ''Computer, could you . . . ah . . . show us what Great-grandpop's place looked like—if it existed?''

''Oh, yes, easily.'' There was a moment of delay; then glassy walls shimmered into view around the group.

"I must caution you that this is a mere optical effect," Genie said. "It represents no substantive referent."

"You may have something here, Case," Chester said. "Computer, I'd like this view firmed up a little—more detail, greater verisimilitude. More realism."

"I'm not at all sure I can manage it, Mr. Chester. It involves readjusting my parameters drastically, which induces a severe electronic itch."

"Try."

"The effort may leave you isolated in a mass-probability environment whose very existence I have every reason to doubt."

"We'll take the chance."

There was a moment of silence. Then:

"There, I've managed tactile quality. You could feel the wall now if you touched it."

"Now add in taste, smell and sound effects. And daub in some externals, too."

After a moment the computer said, "I've extended the effect to include a pseudo-house, with pseudo-grounds, surrounded by pseudo-atmosphere."

"Breathable, I hope?"

"Oh, of course. All my illusions are of the finest quality and extremely accurate."

"In that case, you may proceed to supply the rest of the planet. Take your time and do a good job now."

"That last admonition was hardly called for, Mr. Chester."

"Sorry. But can you do it?"

"Oh, I've already finished."

"So now there's an apparent world outside, resembling the real one in every respect?"

"Yes, indeed; except that it isn't real, of course."

Chester crossed to the door, flung it open. The familiar dusty wine bottles lay quietly in their cradles opposite the reels and flashing lights of the control panel.

"This may not be home," Chester said, "but I think the point is academic."

There was a peremptory rap at the door.

"What's that?"

"A Mr. Overdog of the Bureau of Internal Revenue," the computer answered.

"Well, you asked for realism," Case said. "Shall I let him in?"

"How does he know about this place?" Chester asked.

"Oh, I informed him of it by letter," the computer spoke up. "Retroactively."

"Why? Haven't we got enough trouble?"

"You indicated that you wished the tax problem dealt with. I took appropriate action."

"Say, how much time's passed here while we were out building universes?" Case inquired.

"Seven days, two hours, forty-one minutes and two seconds."

"Shall I let him in, Chester?"

"You may as well."

The door was opened to reveal a lean, red-eyed man with an old-fashioned hat of orange fur covering his hairless head. He eyed Case and Genie.

"I received your letter," he snapped. "Where's Mr. Chester? I trust you're ready to get on with it. I'm a busy man."

"Why . . . ah . . ." Chester started.

More footsteps sounded. A portly man with ice-blue eyes under shaggy white brows puffed into the room.

"Mr. Chester," he began without preamble, "before concluding any agreement with the IRS, I hope you will entertain my offer."

"What are you doing here, Klunt?" Overdog snapped.

"Who's this?" Chester whispered urgently to Genie.

"He's from the Bureau of Vital Statistics," she whispered back. "He got a letter, too."

"When did all these letters get written? There hasn't been time since we remanufactured the world."

"It's remarkable what you can do with temporal vacuoles," Genie said. "The letters were post-marked three days ago."

"What kind of offer did you have in mind, Mr. Ahhh?" said Case.

"Assuming your . . . ah . . . information storage device functions as I've been informed, I'm prepared to offer you, on behalf of the Bureau of Vital Statistics . . ."

"I'll settle for half the tax bill," Overdog cut in. "And we'll entertain the idea of a liberal settlement of the balance, say, over a two-year period. Generous, I'd say. Generous in the extreme."

"Vital Statistics will go higher. We'll pay two

full thirds of the bill!'' Klunt stared at Overdog triumphantly.

"It's a conspiracy! You're playing with prison, Klunt!'' He turned hard eyes on Chester. "Final word, Mr. Chester. Complete forgiveness of the entire tax debt! Think of it!''

"Chicken feed!'' snorted Klunt. "I'll have a check for five million credits ready for you in the morning.''

"Sold!'' Chester said.

"On an annual lease basis, of course,'' Case added.

"Giving us full rights of access,'' Chester amended.

"A deal, gentlemen! I'll revolutionize Vital Statistics with this apparatus! With the increased volume of information, I should say a staff increase of fifty persons would not be excessive, eh, Overdog?''

"Bah! I'll expect your check tomorrow, Mr. Chester—and another next March!'' He stalked out. Klunt followed, planning happily.

"Well, that's taken care of,'' Case said, beaming. "Nice work, Chester, I guess the Wowser Wonder Shows won't have to worry for a while.''

Chester opened the door and looked out. "You're sure it's safe out there, Computer?'' he called.

"The question seems to have become academic, Mr. Chester. A reappraisal indicates that the present scene is substantive after all. Mr. Mulvihill's village was a figment of the imagination, I now perceive.''

"Oh yeah? What about this beard?''

"Psychosomatic," the computer said without conviction.

"What about Genie?" Case asked. "Do we leave her stored here, or what?"

"Genie's coming with me," Chester said.

"Well, I figured maybe she was part of the lease."

"Lease? Nonsense. Genie's as human as I am."

"Don't kid me, Chester. We were both here when she was built—right, Computer?"

"You asked that I produce a mobile speaker in the configuration of a nubile female," the computer replied. "The easiest method was to initate the process of maturation in a living human cell."

"You mean you grew Genie from a human cell—in a matter of hours?"

"The body was matured in a time vacuole."

"But . . . where did you get the cell?"

"I had one on hand—one of yours, Mr. Mulvihill. I took a blood specimen for identification purposes, if you recall."

"But that's impossible. I'm a male!"

"It was necessary to manipulate the X and Y chromosome balance."

"So I'm a mother," said Case wonderingly, "and an unwed mother at that. It figures, though—growing a real girl was simpler than building one out of old alarm clocks."

"In that case," Chester said, taking Genie's hand, "I hope you'll consent to give the bride away in your capacity as both parents—assuming Genie agrees."

"Oh, Chester," Genie said.

"Well, folks," Case boomed, "let's have a drink

and get used to the idea.''

"I'll be along in a few minutes," Chester said. "I want to have a talk with the computer first.''

"What about?''

"I've spent twenty-five years in society and contributed nothing. Now I'm going to start a school—just a small institution for a few selected students, at first. I want to see what I can do to straighten out a few of the world's irrationalities. The computer has the facts—and, thanks to Kuve, I've learned to think.''

"Yep, you've changed, all right, Chester. Well, take your time. We'll wait.''

Chester settled himself in a brocaded chair. "All right, Computer. Here we go with your first lesson: Is-not is not not-is. Not-is is not-is not. Not-is-not is not is . . .''

AWARD-WINNING
Science Fiction!

The following titles are winners of the prestigious Nebula or Hugo Award for excellence in Science Fiction. A must for lovers of good science fiction everywhere!

BEST-SELLING
Science Fiction
and
Fantasy

MORE SCIENCE FICTION!
ADVENTURE